# SHRUNK!
## GHOSTS ON BOARD

# Also By Fleur Hitchcock

*SHRUNK!*
*SHRUNK! Mayhem and Meteorites*

*The Trouble with Mummies*
*The Yoghurt Plot*

# SHRUNK! GHOSTS ON BOARD

## FLEUR HITCHCOCK

HOT
KEY
BOOKS

First published in Great Britain in 2015 by Hot Key Books
Northburgh House, 10 Northburgh Street, London EC1V 0AT

Text copyright © Fleur Hitchcock 2015
Cover illustration copyright © Ross Collins 2015

The moral rights of the author and illustrator have been asserted.

A CIP catalogue record for this book is available from the British Library.

ISBN: 978-1-4714-0346-0

1

This book is typeset in 11pt Sabon using Atomik ePublisher

Printed and bound by Clays Ltd, St Ives Plc

www.hotkeybooks.com

Hot Key Books is part of the Bonnier Publishing Group
www.bonnierpublishing.com

Black Spirit Island

This book belongs to

| Dorset County Library | |
|---|---|
| | |
| **Askews & Holts** | 2015 |
| | £5.99 |
| | |

# Bywater-by-Sea

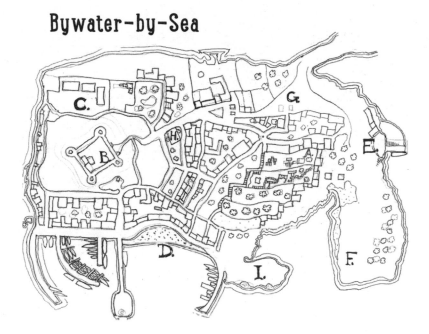

A is the Model Village
B is the Castle
C is the School
D is the Beach
E is the Seawater Baths
F is Mr Burdock's Donkey Field
G is the Edge of the Village
H is the Town Hall
I is North Beach and the Bird Reserve

# Prologue

'Welcome, everyone,' called the tall woman. 'Welcome to Marigold's Island Tours.'

The crowd on the Trusty Mermaid murmured to each other and licked their ice creams. Only one of them glanced across to the bank of cloud that they were approaching, a look of doubt crossing her face. The rest soaked up the glassy blue sea to the south, the warm sunshine dancing across the water, and threw the complimentary floppy hot dogs to the seagulls that played in the wake of the boat.

'We'll moor for a very few minutes on Mystery Smoke Island –'

'Why's it called Mystery Smoke, Miss?' piped up a small girl clutching a plastic pony.

The tour guide ignored her. '– which was the scene of the tragic shipwreck in 1859, when the Golden Unicorn *was bound for Lisbon, and instead –*'

'Did everybody die, Miss? Was it horrible?' asked the girl with the pony.

'Yes. I believe –'

'Was it horrible, Miss? Was there lots of screaming and tragedy, Miss?'

'I don't –'

'Was it because of a sea monster, Miss? Or did a hole open up –'

'Shhh,' said the girl's father, and stuffed a lollypop in her mouth.

'Yes, well,' said the tour guide as sweetly as she could manage. 'D'you know? No one's been for years – this is the first trip within living memory. I've certainly never been.'

'But, Miss –' sputtered the girl with the pony.

'Shall we dock, Captain?' interrupted the tour guide.

The seagulls fled as the boat drifted towards a crumbling jetty that loomed out of the mist. A crewman threw a rope around an ancient rusty bollard and pulled them alongside.

The day trippers hesitated. It was sunny out at sea. Here it was colourless and chill.

'Anyone up for a spot of exploration?' asked the tour guide.

A handful of people teetered along the gangplank and stepped onto the island. Inside the fog, Mystery Smoke Island was even greyer. Everything on it was grey, worn and bony, from the empty bell tower to the gravestones spread along the shore, to the rabbit's skull picked clean by the salt and the wind. Even the thorn bush embedded in the black sand was grey.

'It's ever so cold here,' said a woman, rubbing her bare arms.

'Maybe we should get back on the boat?' said another, hanging her handbag on the wing of a stone eagle that stuck out from one of the graves. She put on her cardigan.

'I . . .' said the guide and paused. She glanced

around at everyone as if there was something wrong. 'Does anyone else feel watched?' she muttered.

'What's that?' said a man, pointing towards the mist on the far side of the island. Something swirled in the whiteness, something dark. The mist parted, as if an invisible person was running through it. As if more than one invisible person was running towards them.

As they stared, an icy wind blew across the island. It cut a path right through the dried grasses in the graveyard, and whisked the fallen leaves into the air. It caught the bag hanging from the eagle's wing and twisted and tossed it. It whipped the island fog and wrapped it around the boat, cutting them off thickly from the blue sea they had just left.

Everything fell deathly silent and very cold.

No one spoke, but the few that had ventured onto the island crowded to get back on the boat, their footsteps muffled and hollow on the wooden gangplank.

Unasked, the crewman slipped the rope from

the bollard and leapt back on deck. The captain revved the engine and swung the boat out towards the open sea, out of the fog.

Everyone leaned forward, hoping they would break out of the cloud any second.

Everyone strained for the sunlight.

But they couldn't reach it.

For an hour they headed west, distant sparkles catching on distant waves, but the fog stayed with them and no matter how the captain steered, the boat remained cold, dark and grey.

'It's as if we picked something up on that island,' said the woman with the bare arms.

'Yes,' said her friend. 'Call me silly, but it's as if we've taken on a spirit.'

'Don't say that,' said the other.

The boat ploughed on in silence for another hour.

Somewhere at the back someone laughed. It was a long, delighted laugh, a wicked laugh.

They all turned to look.

But there was no one there.

No one, but the fog.

# Chapter 1

'That,' says Jacob, beside me, 'is the best idea anyone's had in absolutely ages.'

Eric leans forward and reads out the notice pinned to the telegraph pole. *'Town meeting to discuss the plans for redevelopment of North Beach Nature Reserve and surrounding area. Agenda to include the siting of proposed theme park and Whizzo Builder Corp's commitment to renovation of the seawater baths at South Beach. Plans can be viewed in the library . . .* What?! That's not a good idea at all – it's terrible.'

'Why?' asks Jacob, stuffing one end of a jelly lace between his lips and sucking. 'A theme park would be awesome . . . megatastic . . . amaze balls!' Jacob heaves himself around in a circle, rising and dropping. I think he's trying to be a roller coaster.

'It's where they want to build it – the North Beach Nature Reserve – they can't possibly build a theme park there,' says Eric.

'Whyever not? It's just a load of birds and some mangy scrub. The only people who are going to miss it are twisters, witchers . . . whatever.'

'Twitchers, actually,' says Eric. A single wild curl of his ginger hair bounces furiously on his forehead. 'We're twitchers, and birds are important. Birds are a crucial part of the ecosystem. They enrich our lives and they've as much right to this planet as we have. Theme parks are utterly frivolous, noisy, pointless things.'

'Oooo – ooh,' says Jacob, raising his eyebrows. 'So now, Snot Face is a greeny earth-warrior killjoy as well as a nerd. Well, *you* can spend *your* holidays twitching with a load of stinky birds – some of us like having FUN!' He races off squealing with his arms out.

'Rat-tat-tat-tat, rat-tat-tat-tat,' he shouts. Somehow he resembles a winged gobstopper, but in his mind, he's probably some sort of aeroplane firing on innocent aliens.

'Jacob,' Eric shouts at his back. 'If all you can do is insult me, I'm not going to bother arguing with you. Just accept it this time, you're wrong.'

I'm not sure I've ever seen Eric so cross.

Jacob dances ahead of us, swooping and rat-tatting. We walk on down the hill in silence. The thing is, I sort of agree with Jacob. North Beach is cold, dismal and covered in bird poo. It's a miserable place. I can't actually see that turning it into a theme park would be any loss at all. It would mean there was actually something to do here. As Jacob says, something fun. But I don't like to see Eric so miserable.

I glance back at him. He's wrapped the kite string around his hand so tightly that the tips of his fingers are bright pink. His face is red too.

We stop by the end of the pier. A line of day trippers skitter along the jetty, towards the shore.

'They don't look like they've had much fun,' I say, feeling a sudden shiver down my spine as the last of them passes.

Eric doesn't answer. He rubs his arms and looks angry.

We clamber down to the beach, and Eric holds out the kite as if it might leap from his hands into the sky.

There's absolutely no wind. In fact there's a slight fog, but I can't bear the look on Eric's face so I rush backwards with the string, passing through a strange cold patch of air and step ankle deep into the waves.

The kite stays flat on the pebbles.

'Kites are for babies,' announces Jacob, strolling back towards the pier. 'Tell me when you've had enough running around. I'm going to act my age and go and look at the plans for the theme park in the library – I bet they'll have a Wall of Death.' He crunches over the sand and struggles up onto the sea wall. 'See you.'

I watch his back until he disappears amid the tourists.

Behind me, Eric sighs.

The kite's still lying dead on the beach. I pull the string again, but it refuses to fly.

'It's no good,' he says, sadly, wiping the corner of his eye. Since he and Jacob developed strange powers, I can't tell if he's crying or if he's spouting the spontaneous water that his hands and feet now generate, but just now, I suspect tears. 'It's not going to work.' He sits on the sand, lies back and points at the sky.

A seagull wheels and swoops over the pier. 'A Little Tern,' he says. 'They wouldn't have anywhere to live if North Beach was redeveloped.'

'Oh,' I say, 'surely there's a rock or something?'

'No – they like the shingle ground, so that they can dig out their nests. If they can't have North Beach, the lucky ones will skip up the coast to Bywater Regis and cram in on the tiny bird reserve there. The rest won't bother to come here at all. They'll migrate to somewhere else – or die.'

I glance around for anything that might take his mind off it. A patch of concentrated fog lingers at the end of the beach and, above the cry of the Tern, I can hear some singing. 'Where is it? Where is meeeeee?' comes a thin, flat girl's voice.

But there's no girl, just the captain of the Marigold Tours boat and an anxious-looking tour guide talking to each other and a group of boys licking ice creams.

'Can you hear that?' I say.

'No,' says Eric. 'What?'

I point towards the flickering mist.

'That singing over there.'

'Oh,' says Eric, still watching the seagull. 'It's probably nothing.'

But as I stare into the small patch of whiteness, I see the shape of a top hat, and underneath it, a pair of eyes glinting.

I peer into the mist, expecting it to fade. But it doesn't. I see the eyes and the eyes see me and even though Eric's almost always right, I'm pretty sure they aren't nothing.

# Chapter 2

I can tell which way Jacob walked by the trail of destruction along the high street. Despite the fact that his mouth burns when he uses his powers, he doesn't seem to be able to control them. Outside the fish and chip shop there used to be a huge plastic ice-cream cone. Now it's sagging on one side, and the sign reads *ish and hips*. We catch up with him on the steps of the library. He's enjoying himself, setting fire to things with his fingertips.

'Did we have a nice time flying our kite and talking to the birdies?' he says. He sends a sheet of flame at a postbox door, instantly melting the lock and causing the door to swing open, spewing letters over the tarmac. He clutches his mouth immediately afterwards. I know his tongue will hurt, but even so a broad grin spreads over his face.

'Jacob, you idiot,' says Eric, shooting a flood of water from his palms across the road.

I try and peel escaped letters and postcards from the ground, but they're mostly ruined. 'You need to be more careful.'

'Oh do shut up. It's fun and I'm bored. If they build a theme park I wouldn't be bored, and I wouldn't have to set fire to things. Anyway – why can't I do it?' He releases sparks into the air and pops a passing child's helium balloon. The child bursts into tears, screaming madly at his parents. The younger sister's eyes open wide and she too races away from us down the street, wailing and shouting.

'Because you're upsetting people, and because someone will notice,' I say, pointing at the melted postbox.

'And? What if they do? I can have the recognition I deserve – can't I? I'm a superhero.'

'Superheros don't pop little kids' balloons,' I say.

Jacob swings into the library, ignoring us, and we follow him through the bookcases to stop by the large table in the middle of the room. A man and a woman in matching suits stand by a huge model of a fun fair. There are little roller coasters and bungee jumps and everything you'd expect, perfectly made in white architect-y cardboard with tiny people and tiny trees.

'Gosh – young people! You're just who we need to talk to.' She looks as if she actually wants to eat us, she's so delighted. 'Welcome to the new Bywater-by-Sea theme park design. This is a small version of the real thing, of course,' she says, addressing us as four-year-olds.

Jacob walks around the model. He doesn't look happy and I really hope he's not about to release a shower of sparks over the cardboard.

'So, hang on, is this what you want to build

on North Beach?' Eric looks appalled.

'Oh yes,' says the woman. 'More fun than stinky old birds – eh?'

Eric doesn't answer. He turns away quickly, a mass of hair flopping over his face, and leaves the library. I see him wipe his nose on his sleeve. No one else notices him go.

'So this will be the Bunny Hop café,' says the woman, pointing at a pair of ears sticking out of the model.

'Bunnies?' Jacob curls up his top lip. 'Why bunnies?'

'I think you'll find this goes down very well with the littlies. We've built three of these theme parks before, you know – bunnies, squirrels and chipmunks – all frightfully popular.'

I notice that Jacob's feet have burned two footprints into the nylon library carpet. 'C'mon Jacob,' I say. 'We've seen it now. Let's find Eric.'

Jacob ignores me. 'But where's the fun in bunnies?' he says. 'They're all soft.'

The woman glances anxiously at the man, raising her eyebrows and looking uncomfortably at Jacob, who has begun to send up curls of smoke from his hair.

'Well, young man,' says the man in the suit, coming over. 'We just . . .'

This time I grab Jacob by the arm and drag him out of the library, and a chunk of nylon carpet comes with us. We find Eric sitting on the wall outside, mopping his eyes with the corner of his shirt cuff.

'Well, I don't think much of that,' says Jacob. 'Theme park, yes. Bunny theme park – NO.'

'Any theme park is bad,' says Eric, sniffing. 'But that one's particularly horrible.'

'Agreed,' says Jacob, to my surprise. 'We'll have to make them change it, of course,' says Jacob. 'We can't have the town filled with little kids in rabbit suits.' He shudders and then, recovering from the shock of fluffy things, begins to skip, shedding sparks all the way along the pavement.

Eric gets to his feet and we wander up towards the model village, passing Jacob's earlier areas of destruction and entering a new zone of unburned things.

'Seeing that model of the theme park has left

me feeling quite unwell,' says Eric.

'You know what your problem is?' says Jacob, swinging round. 'You've no spirit of adventure. You're like an old man, Snot Face. Things just need to liven up a bit around here.'

He stamps his foot as if to demonstrate. His eyes flash red and the bag of sweets in his hand flares briefly and melts. 'Ow!' he shouts, throwing them towards a tiny wooden shed in the model village. The shed, doused in burning sugar, lights in a tall column of flame which leaps across to one of Grandma's precious bonsai fir trees.

We all watch as the tree crackles and burns, leaving behind a sad smoking stick of charcoal and a circle of burned grass.

'Like that, you mean?' says Eric.

Tiny balls of whirling smoke whizz up into the sky, exactly like burning icing sugar from a toasted marshmallow. In the smoke I see a green flame, a flickering shape, but I can't quite make out what it is. 'Look,' I say, pointing. 'What's that?'

'Maybe it's like the fog down by the pier,' says

Eric. 'Strange atmospheric conditions today.'

'You're seeing things, Model Village,' says Jacob. 'First sign of madness.'

'I don't think . . .' I start, but a voice sounds in my ear, really close, as if it's in my ear itself.

'We should get away from here,' it says.

I jump. 'What!?'

'What?' says Eric.

'OW! Victor!' says the voice in my other ear.

'That. Didn't you hear it? A voice?' I stick my finger in my ear and waggle it. 'Surely you must have done?'

'And hearing things,' says Jacob. 'Second sign of madness.'

'Yeeeoooooww!' something completely invisible squeals by Eric's feet.

'That,' says Eric, 'is weird. What's going on?'

We all stare hard into the air.

'Can you see anything?' I ask.

'No – but I can sort of feel something,' says Eric, dabbing his arms at thin air.

'This is, at last, something interesting,' says Jacob, leaping upright. 'If there's anything there,

I'll get 'em. I CAN SEE YOU!' he announces, circling Eric and me, protectively. 'AND I'M A SUPERHERO SO I CAN DEFEAT YOU!' He takes the sweatshirt tied across his middle and flaps it like a cape, before throwing the arms around his neck and tying them together. A huge cloud of faintly glittery dust escapes, briefly filling the air and catching the sunlight.

For a second, three figures and a cat appear caught in the dust. Their shapes shimmer in midair, hovering above the model village, and then they disappear, just as fast.

Eric and I stand silent, mouths open.

I try to speak, but all I can do is squeak at the back of my throat. I know that the dust that came from Jacob's sweatshirt is the magic dust from under the castle, but I've never seen it do anything like that before. Not create people out of nowhere.

'But,' says Eric.

Jacob leaps forward to embrace the empty space where the figures were. 'Hey,' he hisses back at us. 'Aliens! They must be aliens.' Then, turning to address the air, he says, 'Where are you from? What planet?' He strikes a Napoleon-pose and says, 'Do you realise how utterly awesome I am?'

The empty space says nothing. No one replies, not even the cat, but something cold brushes my cheek and I notice Eric shiver.

# Chapter 3

'Chips,' announces Jacob. 'What we need after an extra-terrestrial experience like that is chips.'

Jacob joins the queue outside the fish and chip shop. Eric hovers nearby, not exactly joining, not exactly walking away. He's almost certainly thinking about birds.

I stand midway between them, thinking 3 per cent about birds, 3 per cent about theme parks, but mostly thinking about the cold and the mist and the odd people looming out of the glitter. I can't get Eric to concentrate on them – he's miles away with the seagulls.

'Hello boys.' Grandma appears on the pavement, a basket of shopping on her arm. She prods the huge melted plastic ice-cream cone with her toe. 'Nice,' she says. 'Jacob?'

I nod.

She stares at Eric. 'Anything the matter?'

'No,' I say.

'Yes,' says Eric. 'Everything. They want to build a theme park on the bird sanctuary. It's – it's abominable.'

'Oh, that,' says Grandma. 'Don't worry, it's a long way from happening. Surely they can't start until the whole town has agreed.'

Jacob stumbles out of the chip shop, two packets in his hand. 'One for me and one for you two to share – don't say I'm not generous.' He looks up at Grandma. 'You don't want any do you?'

She waves the suggestion away and watches as Jacob squeezes past some railings, rolling his stomach in and out. A sort of tsunami of belly fat that crashes over the top of his jeans. He catches her staring. 'I'm not fat – just well built.'

Grandma shakes her head as if to get free of the vision of Jacob's gut. 'I wonder,' she says. 'I'm sure that the theme park won't be allowed. Everyone loves the bird sanctuary. But I'll have a word with the Worthies – perhaps we need to get a campaign together.'

Jacob stares at her as if she's talking Martian. 'Speak for yourself,' he says. 'I'd much rather have a theme park. Just imagine the possibilities! We could have a daredevil ride, lit with real sparklers, and a roller coaster that takes people right through the sea, underwater with sharks and jellyfish and stuff and exploding hot dogs and boil-in-the-mouth toffee apples and giant inflatable dogs and . . . what are you all staring at?'

I point at his feet. In his enthusiasm he's melted the tarmac, and is now standing ankle deep in the road, squidgy blobs of asphalt bubbling around his trainers.

'Jolly good,' says Grandma. 'Just make sure you take those shoes off before you go through your front door.' She sets off up the hill to the house.

'Grandma.' I catch her up.

'Yes, Tom, dear?'

'Grandma – do you believe in visions?'

She walks another three paces, stops and turns to face me. 'Visions? Tom – what makes you ask?'

'Hypothetical – I mean, I just wondered.' I'm now wishing I hadn't asked – Grandma's got that poking around inside your head expression on her face. She's not going to let it go.

'Has something happened?'

'No – nothing.' I can't actually look her in the eye.

'If by visions you mean ghosts . . .?'

I say nothing and draw a circle in the dust with my toe.

'Because ghosts can be very unpredictable,' she says slowly.

'Oh?' I ask.

Grandma waves the words away. As if she hasn't said them. 'Well – I believe they can be. I've heard it said. Obviously I don't know anything first-hand.'

'Hey! Tom!' shouts Jacob from down the road. 'Don't you want these chips?'

'Remember you can talk to me anytime,' says Grandma. 'Don't do anything foolish though . . .'

'I won't, Grandma,' I say, turning and trotting down the hill. 'I promise.'

# Chapter 4

I find a purple frisbee sticking out of a bin and we take it with our chips down to the castle green.

Eric's terrible at playing any game that involves missiles. So's Jacob. They throw hard but in the wrong direction, and if it's coming towards them, Eric runs away from it, and Jacob just stands there expecting it to stop in his hand.

'Oh come on, you two!' I shout, running the full length of the castle green for the tenth time. 'Make an effort.' But by the time I've reached them, Jacob's thrown himself flat onto the grass and is stuffing chips in his mouth.

'That business in the model village – those people appearing – was great. I loved it,' says Jacob. 'Hey Snot Face, can't you work out what it was?'

Eric takes off his glasses and hangs them over his knee, rubbing his face with his palms. 'I've no idea what caused it – perhaps some change in the temperature causing an alteration of the molecular structure of the air? A hologram?'

'Or perhaps someone around here's got powers we don't know about,' I say.

Jacob sits up. 'Really? Awesome. Who?'

'Half the village has powers from catching meteorites,' says Eric. 'But I don't think I've ever heard of anyone conjuring people.'

'Well, I think we should check for strangers. Perhaps someone here on holiday has managed to develop powers.'

Eric nods. 'Good idea.' He holds a chip in the air, halfway to his mouth. 'But there hasn't been a meteor storm recently. So no one could have picked up a meteorite.'

'Exactly,' says Jacob, a look of incomprehension crossing his face. 'What?'

I listen while Eric explains to Jacob for the millionth time that the person who catches the meteorite develops the powers, but only inside the boundaries of Bywater-by-Sea. And that each meteorite only works for the person that catches it.

While he's droning on, I put my hand up, so that my finger and thumb make an O and frame Jacob's chips. They'd look dead cute, small. I could use my own shrinking power to make a packet of mini chips, but as I look through the gap between my fingers, one of Jacob's chips rises and falls all on its own.

'Did you see that?' I ask. 'One of Jacob's chips moved on its own. I'd swear it.'

Next to me, Eric leaps up and backs towards the castle wall.

'Do you think we've got an invisible alien here?' Jacob hauls himself to his feet, staring hard at nothing. 'That would be awesome.'

I scrabble back, stumbling upright, watching the pile of chips. They don't move again.

'Um,' I say. 'Perhaps it was the wind or something. Anyway, suddenly I don't fancy any more chips.'

'Funnily enough, nor do I,' says Eric. 'And d'you know, you're right. I saw it too. I can't explain it and I don't like it.'

# Chapter 5

We play frisbee with false enthusiasm.

'Aaaaaarghghghghghghhhhhhh!'

'What was that?' yelps Eric, chucking the frisbee over the castle wall. Even Jacob turns pale. We've tried to get rid of the creepy feeling by running around even harder in the sunshine. But no amount of sun has driven it away. I should feel 99 per cent good today, but I don't – it's more like 50 per cent good, 20 per cent bad and 30 per cent slightly worried.

'Aaaaaarrrrghghghghghghghgh!' the scream comes again.

It's an awful sound. Long and distant and old.

'It's the undead,' whispers Jacob.

'Aaaaarghghghghghghghghgh. Ow!'

'Where's it coming from?' I ask.

'The castle, the castle!' Jacob whoops and prances.

'I think he's right,' says Eric. 'Although, it sounds like it's hurt itself,' he says. 'I don't think the undead can hurt themselves.'

'In that case I was right in the first place – it's an alien,' says Jacob, letting off an arc of sparks. 'Let's go into battle, engage them now. It's always much harder to fight aliens once they've established a food source.' He races, dog-like, in a circle. 'Troops, we need a plan of attack. We need to attack the castle. ONWARDS!' He charges ahead, bouncing over the grass and lunging at buttercups.

'We don't need to attack the castle. The gates are wide open. We just need fifty pence to get in,' says Eric, swiping the hair out of his glasses.

'OK then, let's go and investigate.' I shake the last chips out for the seagulls and fold up the paper before jamming it in my pocket.

'You shouldn't do that, you know,' says Eric.

'What? Put chip paper in my pocket?'

'No, give chips to the seagulls. It encourages them to raid bins, which can be a real problem, and besides, chips have no nutritional value. They're not at all good for seabirds.'

'So what are you supposed to feed them?' I say, picking up the chips and jamming them into my pocket too.

'Ideally, hard-boiled eggs and watercress.'

The castle courtyard is empty, except for a small workman's hut and a pile of hazard-warning vests. No one's even on duty in the ticket booth.

'Aaaaarghghghghghghghgh, OW! OW! Blasted cat!' We jump as a strange voice wails across the courtyard.

'We're closer then,' says Jacob.

'Doesn't sound much like aliens,' I say. 'Sounds human.'

'You're right,' says Eric. 'Unless aliens speak English.'

We stop and listen again.

'Ooooooooooooooh, I think I've broken my toe,' the voice wails.

'It's definitely,' I say, 'coming from the entrance to the dungeons.'

We cross the courtyard and stand at the top of the stone steps that lead into the bowels of the castle. *Dungeons. Please be careful, it could be slippy*, says the handwritten sign. It's sunny and warm out here. Inside it's black, and it smells of moss and earth and cold.

'Right,' says Eric, looking at me.

'Yes,' says Jacob.

'Oooooh,' calls the distant voice.

'What's the plan?' I say.

'Perhaps we should get an ice cream before we go down,' says Jacob.

'Good idea,' says Eric. 'Let's get one from the café upstairs.'

Ten minutes later we're standing in exactly the same place, but this time with ice-cream cones. Ice creams make you feel bolder, like you've got a weapon. At the very least you could buy yourself a split second by jamming it in someone's face.

'One, two, three . . . go!' Actually, Jacob and I go and Eric follows a little later.

For the first couple of minutes, I can't see a thing, so I have to run my fingers down the damp walls. But gradually my eyes get used to it and I realise that there are occasional dim, moody lights set into alcoves over small snippets of information. I stop and read one out: *'The Bywater-by-Sea Castle dungeon was used to imprison notorious pirate One-Footed Jack. His boot is said to haunt the corridors.'*

'Great,' says Jacob. 'Bywater-by-Sea's such a dump that it's haunted by a boot.'

'Blast!' comes the voice from the tunnel.

'Did you hear that?' I say.

The other two don't answer, but we stand together, waiting in the gloom before inching forward again.

Eric stops by a dim red lamp and reads out another notice, extra cheerily: *'Mad Angel was a redheaded smuggler who died in the cells,*

*apparently unintentionally poisoned by her gaoler,*
*Josephine Perks.*' He glances at me. 'One of your
ancestors?'

I think about some of Grandma's less lovely
cooking. 'Probably.'

We venture on down the passage. My ice cream
has nearly gone. If I met the voice now it wouldn't
be much of a weapon.

Every now and again, Jacob lets off a spark, which
crackles on the moss, but otherwise we're silent.

Eric touches my arm and I stop.

There's talking coming from down in the
darkness in front of us – a man and a girl.

'But you haven't got any bones,' says the girl's
voice. 'You're a . . .' Then there's a pause and she
says, 'That isn't supposed to happen.'

'Who is that?' Eric whispers to me.

The hairs on the back of my neck leap to
attention.

'Stop whispering in my ear.' It's the man this time.

'Can you see us?' asks the girl.

'I can hear you. Where's that idiot Billy gone?
Why can't I see you?'

We stop in the shadows just before the end of the passage. In front of us are the dungeons, lit with dull red lighting that's supposed to be scary firelight and which is actually just not quite bright enough to see anything properly. They're ancient, drippy, mossy stone rooms with heavy bars across the front designed to stop anyone getting in or out. All the mined dust and rocks from Professor Lee's attempt to steal the castle meteorite are locked inside. Grandma holds the key – she's even heaped the dust up so that it can't be reached from outside the bars. She's thought of everything. It's impregnable. The bars are solid, the padlock's enormous.

But right now there's a man inside.

A man with staring red eyes and a battered top hat. He's holding the bars as if he's arrived inside them by accident, and talking to himself.

'Wow!' whispers Eric.

'Oh!' is all I can think to say. 'Oh,' and, 'How did he get there?'

# Chapter 6

We skulk in a doorway opposite. 'I'm sure he's the same man I saw for a second down on the beach and again in the model village,' I whisper. 'He looks like someone out of a film.'

'A really old film,' says Jacob. 'A black-and-white one.'

'He shouldn't be in there,' says Eric. 'It's dangerous.'

'Well, let's get him out,' says Jacob, marching out of the shadows, his flip-flops slapping on the cobbles. 'Hey!' he shouts. 'That's off limits, that is.'

Although it's gloomy I can see that for a moment the man behind the bars seems to panic, but very quickly he pulls his face into a picture of charm. 'Goodness. People. And you can see me? Oh! How delightful . . . boys.'

'How did you do that?' I ask. 'You're not supposed to be there.'

'Yes,' says Eric. 'Do you have a key?'

'Like this,' says the man, pulling himself tall and jamming his arm and shoulder through a gap in the bars. He strains against the bars, ramming his face into the space between them and wriggling. His head is not going to fit through, one of his ears squishes forward and his top hat crumples but he stays firmly his side of the bars. 'Ow!' he says, pulling himself backwards and rubbing his ears.

'I could have told you that you wouldn't fit,' I say. 'What were you expecting?'

'I don't understand. I just walked in,' he says, shaking the bars. 'A moment ago. It was easy. This is impossible, quite impossible – something ridiculous has happened.'

Jacob laughs. 'Ridiculous? You're ridiculous. Fancy imagining you could get through those bars. Fancy thinking we were so stupid we'd believe you!' He whirls around, his arms outstretched. Sparks scatter from his fingertips and bounce through the dull red glow illuminating everything. They reflect from the puddles on the floor and the dripping walls. They bounce into the darkest corners and everyone looks demonic in the light, especially the man in the cage who can't take his eyes off Jacob.

From nearby, I hear a sharp intake of breath, but there's no one standing there. Once again I get the prickly neck feeling.

'I'm not ridiculous,' says the red-eyed man, grinning madly. 'I'm delighted you've found me. How serendipitous.'

Jacob stops. The sparks stop. He eyes the man in the cell with great care.

'You're really weird, you are,' he says in the end, letting drop a single spark that floats on the air, dancing like a firefly before snuffing out on a puddle with a tiny crackle.

'Marvellous!' says a voice in my ear. 'Marvellous!'

'Flip!' I say. 'Did you hear that? It's that voice again.'

'Yes,' says Eric.

'Come out, wherever you are!' Jacob shouts, spinning around and spraying more sparks across the passage. 'I can see you – hear you – whatever.'

Strange shapes emerge briefly in the light of the sparks, and a reflection glimmers on the puddle. Almost human shapes.

'Can you?' asks the voice. 'Can you really see me?'

'Yes,' says Jacob.

'No,' I say, because I'm not sure if the thing I saw was a person, or a lump in the dungeon wall.

'Maybe,' says Eric. 'I can certainly hear you.'

'Can you do it again? That spark thing – it was . . . lovely.'

'Of course.' Jacob sends another spray of sparks over the puddle. This time I do see the outline of someone reflected in the puddle, but it's so brief and so dark I couldn't really say what he or she looked like, or if there really was anyone.

'I say,' says the man in the cage. 'I rather like you – all of you. I sense that you might prove somewhat interesting. In fact, I think I *know* you're going to prove interesting.'

I stare at his red eyes, flickering behind the bars, and shudder.

All *I* know is that I feel really uncomfortable.

# Chapter 7

'I'm Jacob Devlin,' says Jacob loudly, shifting his weight from foot to foot.

'I'm Flora, by the way,' says the girl's voice from the darkness beside me. She sounds close, but at the same time, distant. Her words are muffled. 'Flora Rose.' She must be really small or really good at hiding.

'I'm Eric Threepwood, and he's Tom,' says Eric. 'Who are you? In there?'

'Oh, let me introduce myself – I'm Victor. So pleased to meet you.' The man sticks his hand between the bars. Jacob shakes it. I stand back, trying to work all this out and feeling anxious. In fact, I'd say about 70 per cent anxious. 'So glad you've come.'

We could run away but the man in the cell is still talking and Eric and Jacob are still listening. 'I'm wondering – Master Devlin, isn't it? – as you're so clever and you can make such wonderful sparks, if you could let me out?' He taps the bars. 'It's just that in the last few minutes, I seem to have become stuck.'

'Is that a good idea?' asks Flora Rose, who seems to have moved to the other side of my head, although I still can't actually see her.

'What do you mean?' I ask.

'She doesn't mean anything – stuff and piffle!' interrupts Victor. 'Now, Jacob Devlin, show me what you can do, you remarkable child.'

Jacob puffs. His ego inflates and he gazes at the lock.

'Don't,' says Eric. 'Sparks . . . dust.'

'Oh yeah,' says Jacob, as if he understands. 'Soz, Vic, can't let you out. Too dangerous.'

So we call the fire brigade.

While we wait, Jacob tells Victor about the theme park, and Eric tells Victor about the birds and I draw pictures in the dust with my toe and think that perhaps we shouldn't tell him anything. I'm also beginning to think that Flora Rose is an invisible person. I've peered into every corner and I can't see her.

'So,' says Victor. 'Have I got this right – you'd like to keep the bird asylum, Mr Threepwood? But you don't care about it, Mr Devlin? You would rather build this fairground of curiosities?'

'Theme park,' says Jacob. 'With rides and –'

'Yes, yes,' cuts in Victor. 'Park of curiosities and whatnot.' He screws up his face in concentration as if he's really interested, but I can't help feeling that, as a total stranger, this is essentially weird. 'So the bird hideout is in some way paramount?'

'Sanctuary,' says Eric. 'Yes, it's terribly important. It's the last refuge of a number of fragile coastal species.'

Victor nods his head. His eyes, still unusually red, cast from side to side. I don't think he's really listening to them. He's thinking about something else and making the right noises, like headmasters do. 'So you need an idea for the preservation of this bird stronghold?'

'We do,' says Eric. 'Quite badly.'

'On the other hand, Bywater-by-Sea is the most tedious place EVER, and we badly need SOMETHING to liven it up,' says Jacob. 'Anything, really. But Snot Face is dead set against the idea of FUN!'

'All I'm doing is thinking of the long term, Jacob,' says Eric.

'Ah yes, the long term,' says Victor, sagely. 'Very important.'

'And I,' says Jacob, letting off a couple of sparklets, 'am thinking of the rest of the town.'

'So you seek a mutually agreeable solution to this conundrum?'

Eric says, 'We do.'

Jacob picks some melted gobstopper from his shorts and jams it in his mouth.

Once again, Victor glances from side to side, this time letting his gaze linger on Jacob. A broad smile spreads across his face. 'I might, just possibly, be able to help you there, young gentlemen. I might have the beginnings of an idea. But stuck in here, I'm not going to be able to help anyone. So get me out, feed me – I'm frightfully keen on cake by the way, and it's been an age since a fine Victoria sponge passed these lips – and let me expand my mind. Oh! And most importantly, let me see more of those marvellous sparks.'

# Chapter 8

It took the fire brigade most of an hour to get Victor out and they kept asking him how he got in.

'Oh dear chaps, it was easy. I just walked through.'

'Pull the other one,' said the giant fireman with the huge bolt cutters.

But Victor didn't have a better explanation.

'Why exactly couldn't I get him out?' asks Jacob, jamming a gobstopper in his mouth.

'Because the sparks next to the dust could have

done untold damage – you might have blown yourself up,' says Eric.

I know I shouldn't, but my heart leaps just a little at the idea of a giant underground firework display with Jacob as the central attraction.

'Well,' says Eric. 'Let's see what Victor has in mind, now that he's out and about.'

'Yes, he seems like someone with a few ideas,' says Jacob.

'I don't know,' I say. 'There's something fishy about him. And I can't work out how he did get in there. The keys are well hidden.'

'He's not as fishy as that disembodied voice,' says Eric.

'The girl?' I say. 'Well, Victor could be a ventriloquist – good at throwing his voice – or perhaps she was a recording of some sort?'

'Hmmm,' says Eric. 'Why would anyone bother to lock themselves in, and then have a recording of a voice outside in the corridor? I mean think about it, Tom. It's not logical. I agree, there's a lot that's unanswered about him, but if he can possibly help with the bird sanctuary, then I'm prepared to give him the benefit of the doubt.'

We're walking back to Grandma's now. Although I'm really doubtful about Victor, Eric's hopes have been raised by him, and I don't like to dash them flat before we've tried every avenue. Personally I'd have left him behind bars, but Eric's usually right about things.

I study Victor as we walk through the village. He looks utterly mad. His clothes are grey and battered, as if someone's been rubbing them with a stone for a hundred years, and he's got sprouty bits of beard and red starey eyes and he's weirdly grey and bloodless. There's this smell of damp wood around him, and mushrooms – a slight whiff of decaying sheds that reminds me of dustbins. I suppose I agreed to take him home sort of hoping that Grandma might turn up.

As we walk back through the village, he keeps on glancing around, checking over his shoulder and then grinning at Jacob like Jacob is some sort of god.

Jacob loves it. 'Why are we bringing him to your house, Model Village?' he says. 'We should've taken him back to mine – we could have played *Sharks v Cup Cakes* on the games box.' He punches the air. 'Awesome.' He turns to Victor. 'Where do you come from, Victor?'

Victor picks a flower and sniffs it, as if he's never seen one before. 'Oh, such fragrance,' he says, ignoring the question.

We walk past a van parked outside the town hall offices. *Whizzo Fairground Projects* it says on the side.

'That's the third one I've noticed today,' says Eric. He sighs.

'What is Whizzy Fairground Projects?' asks Victor, leaping back as a man bounces over the cobbles on a motorbike. 'Good gracious, what a racket!'

'Whizzo are the people who want to build the theme park, on Snot Face's precious bird reserve,' says Jacob, racing around with his arms outstretched. 'By the time we've finished with them, it'll have roller coasters and death rides and death-defying drops – you know the sort of thing. It'll be mega awesome.'

'Oh?' says Victor, raising an eyebrow. 'Awesome, what an interesting word – how . . . excellent.'

He stops for a minute and stares at his hand. He flexes his fingers as if he's never seen them before. 'Is awesome . . . powerful? I mean, would one bow down before awesome?'

Jacob does an inelegant cartwheel. 'Totally. Awesome is like this!' Jacob sends out a bolt of fire that annihilates the village noticeboard.

'Oh yes, that is awesome,' says Victor.

And I wonder just what's going on inside his head.


Back at Grandma's, Victor checks under the kitchen table, looking for something.

'Is that other person – Flora Rose, the invisible girl – with us?' I ask.

Victor looks towards me, a flicker of panic crossing his face. 'I'm not entirely sure. I seem to have lost my ability to see her. Flora Rose, are you there, dear one?'

I hear a tiny gasp, but no one actually speaks and then the kitchen door swings a little and I get the feeling that someone has left the room.

I lean forward to whisper to Eric. 'She's either invisible or she's . . .' And I think of my conversation with Grandma. 'A ghost?'

'Both are, of course, impossible,' says Eric, under his breath. 'And yet . . .' Eric raises his voice. 'So Victor, what's your idea about the birds?'

'Ah – dear boy – well . . .' He examines the jam jar on the table. 'Was hoping to get the lie of the land, as t'were. I feel, as a newcomer to your fine town, that I don't know the full details, so to speak.'

Eric narrows his eyes. 'Do you want to come and see the bird reserve?'

'No, no. I can totally imagine it – birds, seabirds. I've seen quite a few in my time. Lots in fact. You could draw a map of it – that would give me the general notion.'

'Oh, have you lived by the sea?' I ask.

'You might say that,' he says, eyeing Grandma's cooling blackcurrant scones. 'I say, can one help one's self?'

'Sure,' says Jacob. 'I always do. So Victor, tell us about yourself. Are you from round here? Are you really old?' he asks, popping one of the scones into his mouth and showering me with crumbs.

Victor stares intently at the TV. 'I was born at 21 Twissel Street, Tooting Bec, a long time ago, dear boy, an absurdly long time.' He holds his hands out towards the screen. I wonder if he's expecting to warm them. 'Does this have a large lantern inside?' Although he has a smile on his face he doesn't look terribly happy. I'm not sure if he's really fascinated by the telly or avoiding any difficult questions.

'No, it uses electricity. So where *are* you from – recently – not where you were born?' asks Eric. 'Are you a traveller of some sort?'

'Ow!' Something buzzes in my ear, not quite like a fly, more like Chinese whispers. 'Did you hear that?' I say, swiping at the air.

'No, um, not precisely a traveller, more a person that has . . . come and gone.' Victor smiles cheerily as if he's come up with something brilliant and pokes one of the buttons on the TV. 'This light really is quite fantastic. I'd love one of these.'

'It's not a light, it's a television. Haven't you seen one before?' says Jacob. 'Everyone's got a telly but this one's really old-fashioned – no one has big tellies like that any more.'

'How fascinating!' says Victor. 'So do those people live inside that object? Are they your prisoners?' He turns to Jacob. 'Did you put them there with your . . . extraordinary ability?'

Jacob's not listening. He's got one of Grandma's scones embedded in his bubble gum and is trying to separate them. I glance across at Eric. He scratches his chin and pulls up his socks. I glare at him, trying to catch his attention, but he's staring at the tabletop.

'I mean, Jacob, are you the only one who can . . .' Victor waves his arms in an expansive manner, presumably trying to convey sparks. 'Or can you all . . . make fiery things?'

'Wouldn't you like another scone?' I say, helplessly, kicking out at Jacob, just stopping him from saying anything else.

'Scone?' says Jacob. 'I've already got one in my mouth. What are you on about Tom?'

'I . . .' I stare from Eric to Jacob to Victor, desperately trying to think of a way of telling Jacob to keep quiet without telling Victor what I'm telling Jacob to be quiet about. All I come up with is, 'Um.'

And then Grandma comes in.

# Chapter 9

'More paint,' she says, bowling into the kitchen through the back door, crashing and cranging bin lids and flinging wellington boots across the porch. 'I've done six placards, but I need some red pa—'

She stops dead, staring at us one by one and fixing on Victor. 'What's going on – and WHO ARE YOU?'

He leaps to his feet, bows deeply and a wide smile sweeps over his face. 'Dear lady, Victor Isabella De Macoy at your service.'

'Don't you dear lady me! What are you doing in my kitchen?'

Victor isn't remotely worried by Grandma – in fact he seems livelier now that she's appeared, as if she might be some kind of adversary. 'These charming young urchins invited me in. They rescued me from the castle in fact, and brought me here for' – he waves at the scones – 'sustenance. Are these your superior bakes?'

'Rescued?' says Grandma, dropping her paintbrush in the kitchen sink.

'Yes,' I say. 'Victor was INSIDE the cell at the end of the dungeons.'

Grandma takes off her rubber gloves and turns to face him. 'Were you indeed? And how did you get in there?'

Victor shrugs. He does a very good innocent face. 'I don't know. I just walked in – it didn't seem to be an inconvenience.'

'He's going to help us with the theme-park-versus-bird-park problem,' says Jacob.

'Is he indeed?' Grandma strolls over and circles around him, sniffing and poking. She stops behind his back and sniffs really strongly. 'Graveyards,' she says. 'I smell graveyards.'

Victor wriggles his shoulders and laughs. He doesn't actually say anything.

'Well, you can't stay here,' she says. 'We haven't the room.'

'He can stay at mine,' says Jacob, flicking a spark towards Grandma. 'My mum and dad won't mind.'

'If you say so, dear,' says Grandma, staring into all the corners of the room. 'I have a feeling there are a couple more here like you . . . Anyway, Mr Victor, just so you know, this village is not what you think. Not a sleepy seaside little isthmus, more a cauldron of hidden talent.'

She turns back to the sink, pries the lid off a tin of paint and walks back to the garden door. 'Remember Tom, remember what I said earlier – and take care.'

She goes out of the door and I watch her back as she disappears off to the tool shed.

'What does she mean?' Eric asks. 'About what I said earlier?'

'Dunno, not much,' I say, remembering her words. *Ghosts can be unpredictable.*

'Oh!' Eric cries, jumping away from the table.

'Sugar – how did that get there?' He reaches for a damp cloth and clears it off the tabletop. 'How surprising.'

Something that could be a snarl crosses Victor's face before he replaces it with the charming smile and renews his interest in the television.

'So,' says Tilly, sitting on the kitchen table. 'I was rearranging my bedroom, my new, gorgeously-redecorated-no-old-pieces-of-Grandma's-furniture bedroom. Sorting out my Woodland Friends and punishing the ones who wouldn't stand up properly. When something came in.'

She widens her eyes and looks around us as if we should all fall down in amazement.

'And?' I say.

Tilly screws up her face. She's irritated. I'm obviously not sufficiently impressed.

'It was an invisible person.'

No one even gasps.

'Whaaat?' She stares at us all. 'I mean, how

many invisible people have you ever met?'

'Not very many,' says Eric. 'How do you know it wasn't the wind or something?'

'Because it spoke,' says Tilly, nodding her head. 'It was a girl and it spoke to me, just me.'

'Flora Rose?' says Victor, moving slightly sideways. 'Are you here?'

'How did you know?' says Tilly, disappointed. 'She appeared in my bedroom.'

'We came together,' says a girl's voice straight out of the middle of nothing. This time, everyone does gasp. I mean, it's startling when a voice comes out of nowhere. It's disturbing. 'I asked her for a mirror – I told her I was a ghost and she told me about everyone's powers.'

'Powers?' says Victor.

'A ghost!' says Jacob.

'And,' Tilly says, helping herself to a family-size packet of crisps, 'did you know there are *three* ghosts here? Yes.' Tilly is obviously enjoying her moment of importance. 'My friend, Flora Rose –'

'The voice,' interrupts Eric.

Tilly glares at him. 'Yes, the voice. And she

says there's another one, Billy, who we can't see and we can't hear because he hasn't learned to throw his voice like Flora Rose can but who could be standing right next to you.' Everyone jumps, including Tilly. 'And that he,' she points at Victor, 'is a ghost too – except, he's been changed in the castle dungeon, somehow.'

'Me? A ghost? How preposterous!' Victor laughs and turns beetroot. 'I'm just a traveller, an innocent traveller.'

I look across at Victor. It would explain his greyness and how he got inside the bars. And it would explain his age – the fact that he looks Victorian, or even older. And it would explain Grandma – she must have guessed.

'There's also a cat,' says Tilly. 'Called Jim or something?'

'Shipwreck James,' says Flora Rose. 'He's Victor's cat. Horrible creature, aren't you?' Flora Rose's voice goes silly, and although I can't see her I imagine she's doing that cootchy-coo thing that people do to babies. Something on the floor makes a laid-back yowling sound. 'Tiddly tiddles.

Yes, I'd like to eat sardines too . . .'

If you pretend it's on the radio, it's OK. If you imagine it's a ghostly girl talking to a ghostly cat in your grandma's kitchen, it's less OK.

'So the thing is,' Tilly's talking again, 'I want to go – and Tom, you can take me.' Her lower lip is jutting out so far that she could balance a whole box of chocolates on it.

'Where?' I ask, wondering what she's been talking about.

'Mystery Smoke Island, stupid,' she says. 'It's where they come from.' She waves her finger in the air.

We all turn and stare at Victor.

'Is this true?' I say. 'Are you really a ghost?'

'Piffle! Stuff and nonsense! Don't believe a word of it,' he says, shaking his head.

There's a long silence.

'Victor,' says Flora Rose.

'Oh – all right. Yes, I suppose I am. I was. And I lived on the island with her, and him.' He waves his hands in the air. 'Wherever they may be.'

His words echo round the kitchen. I stand,

blinking, trying to think what he said and what that means.

'And I want to go there,' says Tilly, folding her arms.

'Why, my sweet, would you want to go there?' asks Victor. 'It's dark and dismal, and . . .' – his face falls – '. . . gloomy. Although . . .' He gazes out of the window as if something has occurred to him.

'Because it's spooooooooooooooky,' says Tilly. 'I've never been anywhere full of ghosts, and I want to go and, Tom, as an older brother, my protector, you should want to come with me. In fact,' – she jabs me with her finger – 'if you don't come, I'll go anyway, and I'll probably die there and you'll wish you'd come because you'll be haunted by eternal guilt.' She smiles. 'I'll make a raft and go there all by myself – and drown all by myself, forlorn and lost on the wild stormy seas.'

I'm thinking of ghosts, but Tilly won't let me admit it. She always says these things in public, so I have to answer her. 'I don't even know where Mystery Smoke Island is!'

'I do,' says Jacob. 'I can take you on my Speedmaster 2000 if you like. It's down by the lighthouse. Yip yip!' He races around in a circle making engine noises and swinging an imaginary wheel. 'We're going to a haunting!'

'Really?' Tilly looks at Jacob. 'Does it go fast?'

'Mega fast,' says Jacob.

'And can you steer it?' asks Tilly, doubtfully.

Jacob doesn't exactly answer.

'And – you see, Tom,' says Tilly, looking back at me, 'I was hoping you and your swotty friend might come along too,' she says, pointing at Eric. 'If he can stop staring at the sugar.'

I turn around to see Eric examining the tabletop, his forehead creased into lines. 'I cleaned this up a minute ago. What's going on? There's a D and possibly . . .'

'It's Billy,' says Flora Rose's voice from the middle of the room. 'He's writing something.'

Eric pulls his arm back as if he's been electrocuted. 'Where is he? What does he want to say?'

'Oh la, la, la – silly Billy – let's not worry about that,' says Victor, loudly, sweeping his arm through the sugar. 'Let's get outside in the fresh air. I've an idea.'

'What is it? Have you thought of a solution?' asks Eric. 'Can we save the bird reserve?'

'Dear boy, these things take time. The best plans cannot be hurried. My mind needs to mull and mingle and process the ideas. I think I could take a productive look at the existing bird salvation, wherever it is. And I'll come along to Mystery Smoke Island – it might aid my thinking process. And while we do that, you can tell me all about the lovely things you can all do, or Flora Rose can, if she knows on which side her bread is buttered,' he says, glaring into space.

'None of this sounds like a good idea,' I say, but slightly too late as I watch Victor, Tilly and Jacob stomp out of the front door.

'Flora Rose?' says Eric. 'Are you there?'

But there's no answer, not even the creak of a door or the yowl of a cat, and wherever the invisible Billy is, apparently he's not playing with the sugar any more.

# Chapter 10

'I do hope his plan is good,' says Eric, jamming his foot into his trainer.

I grab my Field Craft backpack and rush outside, watching to see where the others have gone. 'This trip doesn't feel like a good idea to me,' I say. 'I don't want to go there, but Tilly's insistent, and I don't think we should leave Victor here on his own – so he's going to have to come too.'

Eric fiddles with his laces.

'Do you think he's really going to help?' I ask.

'I think we have to give him the benefit of the doubt. I can't stress how serious this is, Tom,' he says. 'Without the bird sanctuary, Bywater-by-Sea will become an ecological desert.'

'But he hasn't actually suggested anything.'

'No – but what have we got to lose? It's just a little trip to the island. What can go wrong?'

Jacob and Tilly have raced on down towards the lighthouse, and Victor is following more slowly, apparently examining everything as he passes.

Catching up with them means passing through the bird reserve. We clamber over the low fence and Eric stops to look at a pile of twigs that might possibly be a nest, although it might equally be random rubbish.

'Little Tern nests,' he says, pointing at the twigs.

'How interesting,' says Victor, glancing at the sticks, his eyes quite cold and uninterested, before looking up towards Jacob and smiling. He strides out over the shingle to catch up. Leaving Eric and me behind.

A large shiny car crackles over the stones and comes to a slow halt on the other side of the reserve. It's the man and the woman from the library. They're obviously drawing up plans because they sling a long tape measure between them and spend a lot of time staring at a map.

'Oh look,' says Eric, gloomily. 'We've had it. There's no point in your grandma protesting now. They're already practically building the wretched thing. Victor really is our last chance.'

'Yes,' I say, watching the man struggling on the cobbles in his town shoes and then looking round towards Victor, who, far from looking at the birds, is chattering away to Jacob and Tilly. 'I'm sure he'll think of something.'

'Hmmm, let's hope so,' says Eric, speeding up and almost running down to the lighthouse. I watch him jog awkwardly over the stones. I wish I could think of a way round the redevelopment. It's making him so miserable and he's been such a good friend. But most people in the town will want a theme park, and in all honesty only a handful of people have any idea about the birds. And a theme park would be fun. I let myself think about the thrill of whizzing down a roller coaster and feel immediately guilty.

Eric really loves his birds and I'm sure he's right, they're almost certainly worth preserving. It's just that I can't think how and I don't for one minute think Victor's going to help.

It turns out that Jacob doesn't really know how to steer the Speedmaster 2000. After we've packed ourselves in to it, and it really isn't a very big boat, we immediately bump into the angry water-taxi driver, and while reversing out of that one, we clunk a small white yacht leaving a long red streak down the side.

'Oops,' says Jacob, pushing away with the boathook.

'Shouldn't we leave a note? Explaining?' says Eric. 'Offering to pay for the damage?'

'Why on earth would we do that?' says Jacob, heading for clear water.

We chug out of the harbour mouth. I'm braced for more scrapes. The nearest object is a small lump of concrete marked by a tall green stripy pole. It's the only thing in front of us and, I would have thought, quite easily avoided, but Jacob heads straight for it.

'Jacob!' I yell over the sound of the straining engine.

'What?' he shouts.

I point frantically at the fast approaching pole. This looks as if it could be about 95 per cent bad.

'Scaredy cat!' he shouts back and throws the wheel to the right, veering violently and throwing Eric and me right across the boat. The manoeuvre bounces us so that a wave caused by our own wake washes over the side and soaks me and, a millisecond later, Eric. Tilly hoots with delight.

'Faster, faster!' she shouts.

I honestly didn't think the boat could go any faster, but it picks up speed and we lurch from side to side until we're properly outside the harbour.

I look around to Victor. He's crouching on the floor of the boat, his coat pulled up over his shoulders. I can't actually see his face. I don't think he likes water much.

'Go, Jacob,' shouts Tilly again. 'Faster!'

There isn't any faster, but it's about then that I realise that the water around my ankles is coming from the bottom up, rather than the top down, and that the little boat is sinking.

'Dad'll kill me,' shouts Jacob, swimming hard for the shore and waiting for no one.

'We'll drown first,' I splutter, groping for a wooden oar and hanging on. 'Are you all right there, Eric? Tilly? Victor? And is that cat with us?'

'No, Shipwreck James stayed on shore,' calls Flora Rose from above.

I tread water, watching the boat turn over and rest, upside down. I'm not sure, but there appears to be a hole in the bottom, which is odd, because there can't have been one when we set off, or we would have sunk much earlier. Tilly's clinging to the side, but her head is only just above the water.

'Tom,' she wails. 'Help me!'

'You can swim can't you?' I say, helping Eric to get to the oar.

'Yes, but I'm weak, and not as strong as you, and I've never been in a boat accident before – I need rescuing. I feel faint and feeble and . . .'

I reach out for her hair with my free hand. It's not that I want to hurt her, but it is a ready-made rope – lots of it and well attached.

'Ow! Tom!' she screams, batting at me and suddenly remembering how to swim.

'Can't you use your powers?' shouts Victor, bobbing up and down, clinging to his battered top hat. 'Can't you do anything? Jacob, you must be able to do something?'

But Jacob's already too far away to hear him.

I think for a moment. I don't imagine that there's anything helpful that I could do, and Eric would only make us wetter.

'Oh, I could do something,' says Tilly, puffing along beside me.

Which is how we end up swimming back into the harbour on a giant pink sparkly oar.

'So it's not just Jacob who can do remarkable things,' says Victor, dripping onto the quayside.

'And exactly what gives you the power?'

'Oh that's easy,' answers Tilly. 'We all caught meteor—'

I deliver a sharp kick to her shin. I don't agree with physical violence, but sometimes it's necessary. Especially with someone as dense as Tilly.

'To-om!' she says. 'Ow-wa! That really hurt.'

I smile at her. 'Sorry, I must have missed my step. Gosh – look, Jacob's breaking in to the Marigold Tours boat. We'd better hurry or we'll miss the trip.'

Tilly narrows her eyes. 'What are you up to, Tom?'

'Did you say meteorites?' says Victor. 'What –?'

But I don't give him time to ask, bundling Tilly along the jetty in front of me and pushing her onto the boat. 'Shhhh,' I say, in the split second that Victor takes to follow us. 'Don't tell him – he's really –'

'Untrustworthy?' she interrupts. 'Yes, I know – isn't it fun?'

# Chapter 11

About a minute after the engine starts, it stops again. It won't work, and we reassemble on the quayside, dripping. I'm actually getting quite cross with this and sit soggily on Tilly's giant inflated oar – which is by now not so giant, nor so inflated – watching a puddle form around my feet.

'Perhaps we're not meant to go,' says Eric, squeezing water out of his T-shirt. 'Perhaps we're supposed to be organising the campaign for the preservation of the bird sanctuary back here with the Worthies and your grandma.'

'A helicopter?' asks Jacob. 'Anyone got one?'

'What a shame! I haven't – whatever a helicopter is,' says Victor. 'Why don't we go back to your house, Tom, and you can all show me your wonderful abilities?' He nudges me. I don't much like being nudged by a ghost, even if he looks like a man. A grey grubby sort of man, with slightly see-through skin. I shuffle further along Tilly's giant oar until I'm teetering on the edge. It tips, spilling Victor onto the ground.

'But I thought you had an idea?' says Eric. 'And that going over to the island would help crystallise that idea?'

'Nice use of vocabulary, my boy,' says Victor. 'But here, or there, I can think, and garner and gather and put together all the little details of your lives – I mean, the life of the town, so to speak.'

'Quite,' I begin, but I stop. Something's, or somebody's, writing a message in water on the stone by my feet. *Don't* – but then it runs out, because the D starts to evaporate.

It's a most peculiar feeling. I watch as the letters form again. It must be Billy. He must be trying to tell me something, but I'm not getting enough at once.

'We could swim,' says Tilly, watching the giant oar shrink back to its usual size. 'I could make a giant rubber ring.'

'Or we could build a raft?' says Jacob.

'How come you ghostly people can't summon a shipwreck from the bottom of the sea? One that would take us over the water?' says Tilly.

'Yeah, that would be neat, with a skeleton crew!' Jacob sits down on the quayside. Gentle steam rises from his shoulders and I notice that his clothes are almost dry.

'Why don't you, Tom and Eric take Tilly to the island?' says Victor. 'Flora Rose and Billy can go with you and I can stay here with Jacob.'

'What about the bird reserve in all this?' asks Eric.

'No,' says Tilly firmly. 'We all go.'

'Yes. We're a team,' says Jacob, putting his arm out in front of him and galloping around behind it.

Something flickers at the side of my vision.

'Billy?' I say quietly.

A Y appears on the stone.

I look back down at my feet. 'Dang,' it says.

'Danger?' I whisper.

I feel a cold finger against my skin, and once again the letter Y appears, on my arm this time. And despite the sunshine that should be warming my back, a shiver as cold as anything I've ever felt races down my spine.

'I can't believe they're really ghosts,' I say to Eric as we huddle inside the bow of the *Trusty Mermaid* alongside the day trippers.

We're sheltering here because about a minute after we'd all decided to go home, the *Trusty Mermaid* pulled into the pier quay and Jacob and Tilly raced off to climb on board. We had to follow. Unfortunately.

'They can't be,' says Eric. 'But you're right, they are. And that Victor – I'm beginning to think he's stringing us along. He's got no intention of helping out with the bird reserve, has he?'

I nod, desperately grateful to see that Eric is finally getting the point. 'How did Grandma know he was a ghost? And she seemed to be able to see Flora Rose and Billy – she knew they were there.'

Eric sighs. 'She's either an Indigo – a person who can see ghosts – or she can smell them or something. I don't know. I don't know everything – OK?'

'OK,' I say. I can tell that he's cross, that he feels let down, that he'd rather be back in the village waving placards about bird sanctuaries, but I'm glad he's here.

I look around to see if I can see any sign of Billy and Flora Rose, but if they are with us, they're keeping very quiet and invisible. Jacob's up on the bow of the ship, studying the horizon. He looks very excited. I am not very excited. If it wasn't for the presence of Victor, Grandma's warning and Tilly's emotional blackmail, I wouldn't be here.

I squeeze some water from my shorts.

Eric sighs, staring past a squabbling family to the waves beyond.

'He definitely made a hole in the bottom of the boat,' I say. 'There was one when we sank, but nothing beforehand. And why did that other boat start and stop? I'm guessing it was Victor pouring water in the tank or something.'

Eric doesn't answer.

'Have you had the messages on your arm?' I ask.

Eric nods.

'Creepy, aren't they?' I say.

He nods again.

'Eric, are you listening?'

'Hmm, yes.' He turns to me. 'Messages, creepy. Victor bad – that sort of thing.'

'But you're thinking about birds.'

He sighs. 'I was remembering a Cormorant, diving into the shallows off North Beach early last August. It was stunning.'

'Right,' I say. 'Well, I was thinking about Victor. It's only a matter of time before he discovers that there are loads of people in Bywater-by-Sea with strange powers and I can't imagine that he's going to use that for any good at all.'

I look over to Victor. He's hunched against the wheelhouse, watching a snotty baby eat a chocolate ice cream. The disgust on his face is so strong that I'm surprised the baby hasn't burst into tears. A woman hands him a camera and asks him to take a picture of her and the baby. At which point the baby notices Victor and begins to scream.

'Yes,' says Eric. 'I suppose you're right.'

# Chapter 12

I'm worried about Eric's lack of interest. Surely he now sees that Victor's dangerous, even without the disturbing Billy messages, and I'm still thinking about it as the boat pulls into the milky fog surrounding Mystery Smoke Island.

'What's that awful smell?' I ask. 'It's like drains.'

'The island,' says Victor. Mournfully. 'It smells hideous – mouldy.'

'Oooh, are we nearly there?' says Tilly. 'Is it here? In this fog?'

'Anyone for Mystery Smoke Island? We only dock for a moment, so could you get yourselves to the forward exit – thank you. We'll pass again at dusk – if you're not on the quay we'll assume you've made your own way back.' The captain's voice is muffled by the mist, but we all shuffle to the front, Tilly jumping up and down with excitement, craning to see the island emerge from the fog. Jacob is bouncing beside her.

All I can actually see is a broken wooden jetty and the ruined spike of a tower poking out of the cloud. All the details have disappeared in the mist.

The boat thuds into the landing stage and as soon as we've stepped ashore, it turns and heads back out to sea. None of the other passengers disembark and we're left alone on the crumbling boards.

No one says anything as the last little square of colour disappears into the grey and the final chug of the engine fades out to sea. A wave washes gently up to the landing stage and plips back, leaving dead-calm water.

'Whoooo, spooky,' whispers Tilly, tiptoeing to the end of the jetty and standing on a patch of sooty black ivy.

'Yes,' I say. I look back to the swirling fog hanging over the sea. I can't see anything of the boat. I can't immediately see any way of getting off the island.

Victor walks off the jetty, picks his way through a groaning metal gate and sinks down to sit on a gravestone. He lets his head sag onto his hands and stares gloomily at another stone, one carved with skeletons, apparently writhing in agony. 'I can't believe I'm back on Mystery Smoke Island,' he says and sighs. He raises one of his hands in front of his face. It might be my imagination, but I think I can see through it.

Beside me, Eric pulls a soggy map from his pocket and arranges it on the wooden planks of the jetty. It's very ancient and very wet.

Everyone stays very still, as if we're all waiting for something to happen.

Distantly, a low howl builds. Not like a wolf – more like wind in the trees. It rises and falls, rushing up towards us and then turning and racing away. I jump. 'What *is* that?'

'The Evergone Forest.' Victor raises his head.

'It's in the dark heart of the island. Dismal, isn't it?'

'Does it do it all the time?' asks Tilly. I detect a very slight lessening of enthusiasm in her voice.

'Almost,' says Flora Rose out of nowhere. I try not to leap out of my skin but I'm still not used to the way she does it. 'Sometimes it goes quiet for nearly long enough for you to forget about it. Then it gets loud and shouty again. It's horrible to live with.'

'Really?' says Jacob, his voice unusually high. It's the first time he's spoken since we saw the blackened stumps of the island emerging through the fog. In fact he's not been remotely superhero-like. Since we left Bywater-by-Sea, not a single spark's leapt from his fingertips. 'Why's it Evergone?'

'No one's ever come back from there,' says Flora Rose. 'Some explorers disappeared in the 1920s. We never saw them again, which was a shame. They were quite fun. They had a fire and sang songs.'

I shiver. I can see that a fire on this island would make it much more bearable. Some light would help.

Flora Rose is still talking. If I listen to her carefully, I can work out where she is, and then it's just possible to see her shape because it's the space the mist doesn't occupy. She's about my height and next to her is a smaller figure who appears to be clinging to her arm. It must be Billy. 'It's also called the Fearful Forest because of the terribly afraid faces on the trees. I think some of them were once ghosts,' says Flora Rose. 'It's not wind in the trees – it's screaming you can hear.'

'Screaming?' says Jacob, shivering. 'I'm not sure I can stand too much of this.' He's standing with his back to the sea. I suppose it's like standing with your back to the wall.

'Then you'll understand why I chose to leave,' says Victor. 'Anyway, chaps – Jacob, old fellow, light us a fire and tell me a spot about the meteorites, eh? Who's got them?' His eyes widen and a long smile creases his face. 'And what do they do?'

'Don't, Jacob,' starts Eric, slightly too late to stop Jacob who looks infinitely more cheerful now the topic of conversation has moved away from ghosts.

'Meteorites. We get powers depending on where they land. We've all got different powers. Tom can . . . Ow! Snot Face, why'd you kick me?' Jacob hops around clutching his leg.

'Oh, this is boring! Can I see the forest?' interrupts Tilly. 'Can we go there? Sounds spooooky.'

'I disagree. This meteorite thing sounds very interesting,' says Victor, looking better, but still a little see-through. 'And here the fog's so thick you can't even see a hundred yards. Let's go back to that nice place you're from, so much warmer, and you could show me your pretty space rock and we can eat more heavenly cake.'

'Oh, I think he's right,' says Flora Rose. 'I know I brought you here, Tilly – but now we're back, I don't feel at all good about this. Can't we go over to the mainland? It was so nice. And really this place is so dark.'

'Ooh,' says Tilly. 'Look at the seagulls! Aren't they weird?'

86

'We keep our meteorites in our – Geddof!' yells Jacob at a large gull which seems to be stalking him. 'Pockets. Go away, you foul creature.'

Victor grabs Jacob by the elbow. There's a sort of a tussle while Victor forces Jacob upright, and Jacob sags. Jacob's sweatshirt gets hitched over his belly, the seagull flies off and Victor straightens up his top hat, a large grin spreading over his face. 'How wonderful!' says Victor.

Wonderful that the seagull flew away? Or wonderful that Jacob keeps meteorites in his pocket? I look again. Victor definitely has something in his hand. I can see because the hand is more transparent than solid and there's definitely something extra in his palm.

'Jacob, Victor – I saw that!' I say.

'What?' says Victor.

'That! You took something out of Jacob's pocket – it's in your hand.'

Victor splays his hands, opens his jacket. I can't see anything and feel really stupid.

'Tom,' glares Jacob. 'Guests – be polite.'

'But –!'

'It's nothing,' says Victor, turning his back on Jacob and heading towards the end of the jetty.

I whisk my meteorite from my pocket into my backpack. I don't know what he's done with Jacob's stone, but he definitely took it. Not that Victor would be able to use mine – because it only works for me.

But I suppose he doesn't know that.

And I don't know for sure that Jacob and Eric's meteorite only works for them.

I'm still staring at him, wondering how he did that, and how to get the meteorite off him, when Tilly grabs my backpack. 'I'm going this way,' she says, yanking the torch off the side. 'Do any of you scaredy cats want to come with me?'

'Don't!' shouts Flora Rose from alarmingly close. 'That's Vile Lucy's place, Ghost Lane. She'll . . .'

But Tilly's already stomped off into the mist. She's already invisible.

# Chapter 13

All the way along the path Victor skulks at the back, muttering. I can only assume that he's trying to make the meteorite work and even though I'm fairly sure he can't, I'm worried that because we're on a haunted island, and because he's really a ghost, something might have changed. He's obviously interested in Jacob's power. He hasn't actually seen Eric's or my powers, and I can't help feeling that he wants Jacob for himself, that he's only come along to keep Jacob within his grasp . . .

That he might, at any minute, get rid of the rest of us.

How did Grandma know that Victor was a ghost? It bothers me. Just like she said that thing about them being unpredictable. It's all making me feel sick.

I'm feeling, maybe, 3 per cent good about this. I know I've got Eric but he's not really using his mind. It's like having half an Eric – the legs, arms and hair half but not the brain half.

At the front of the group Flora Rose squeals.

'What's the matter?' Eric asks her.

'It's Vile Lucy. She's prodding me with a bodkin. STOP IT!' Flora Rose bellows. 'Oh, can't we go back now?'

'Who *is* Vile Lucy?' asks Eric, but Flora Rose doesn't answer and Tilly marches ahead so we all have to follow her into the grey fog.

'I don't like this,' says Eric beside me. 'We shouldn't be here.'

'Well, if you hadn't been taken in by him in the first place we wouldn't be,' I say. 'And now – we've got Tilly involved. She's my sister – but if *you* want to go back . . .'

Eric shakes his head. 'I'm sorry. I know you

don't want to be here either, but I wouldn't abandon anyone. That would be dreadful.'

We press ahead, long flappy things brushing against our faces in the gloom, other things crunching under our feet and all the time the terrible moaning and groaning ringing around our heads. I'm trying to think warm, comforting thoughts – pies and cakes and sweets and crazy golf and smiling holidaymakers, but it's really hard and the terrible moaning just makes it worse.

'What is that?' says Jacob, pointing at a large, leafless tree. Its branches look more like fingers than wood. It's sticking out of a grey porridgy swamp, but it appears to be flexing gently as if it was alive.

'Nice tree,' says Tilly, her voice laden with sarcasm.

'Interesting,' says Eric. 'I've never seen a tree of the genus *Handus* looking so big and healthy.'

The tree seems to move to face us. It might be a trick of the light, but there isn't any light so I'm inclined to think it's the tree itself. I lift my hand and form a ring between my finger and thumb, making an O around the tree itself. From this distance I could shrink it into something quite tiny and harmless.

*Click*, I say in my head.

But nothing happens. I look down at my palm – no tiny *Handus* tree appears and the one in the porridge swamp looks just as big and just as scary as it did.

'It takes people,' says Flora Rose, panting heavily in my ear. 'And ghosts. Actually, it's got Vile Lucy, right now.' The tree squeezes its branches together and Flora Rose gasps. 'That was nasty. Although, perhaps losing Lucy's a good thing. Last year, it took Flat George. He wasn't terribly bright but even so, it seemed a bit harsh. It's a horrible place.'

Jacob picks up a broken tree branch, leans forward over the swamp and offers it to the tree. The tree grabs it immediately, pulverising it and dropping it into the pit at its feet. 'Woah!' says Jacob, leaping back from the side.

'OK, I'll avoid the tree,' says Tilly, looking at it with respect. 'This way, I think,' she says, stomping off down another dark path.

'Tilly!' I shout. 'Tilly, can't we go home?' But she ignores me.

I watch the tree crushing a twig and try once again to shrink it, but it doesn't work.

I'm staring at my empty palm when Victor brushes past – he's bent over and definitely transparent. He appears to be floating over the path, he isn't making footprints and there's something in his see-through pocket. Almost certainly Jacob's meteorite, although it might not matter at all because, so far as I can see, our powers don't work here. This is fine in terms of Victor, but not at all good when it comes to being stuck on an island with a load of haunted things.

Tilly bumps to a halt outside a broken, blackened tower.

'Ah,' says Victor sadly. 'The bell tower. Once so fine, and now so . . .'

'Rubbish?' asks Tilly. 'Is that the word you were looking for? Can we go inside? It looks extra specially spooky.'

'Really?' says Eric. 'Can't we just pretend we've been in? It doesn't look safe.'

Jacob pulls something out of his bag and a powerful beam of light plays over the charred bricks of the tower. 'Wow!' he says. 'Awesome. My Dreamcaster torch is the brightest thing on the island – it's virtually the sun.'

'Extraordinary,' says Eric. 'To be so burned and yet still be standing.'

'It was Oswald that did it,' says Victor, his voice dismal.

'No it wasn't,' says Flora Rose. 'It was Billy that got caught in the fire.'

'Whatever,' says Tilly. 'How d'you get inside?'

'Well, you'll have to put the arm back on that statue to open the door,' says Flora Rose. She points at a sad black marble figure, swathed in more black marble drapery. One arm points up at the sky. The other lies on the ground. Like many things on the island, it's vaguely disconcerting.

'How do you know? I thought you couldn't touch things,' I say.

'How do we know it's not a ghostly trap?' asks Jacob.

'Mr Chenkov, the Russian ghost, could do it for a while, until he blew away on the wind,' says Flora Rose. 'But if you don't want to find out, I don't care. Ugh! Spiders. I hate spiders. You could probably burn your way through the door,' she says to Jacob.

'How come there aren't any other ghosts here?' asks Tilly, picking up the arm and locking it into place.

'There are,' says Flora Rose. 'In fact right now, little Larry, the hurricane boy, is standing next to you looking at your feet.'

Tilly side steps and we all stare at her cherry pink trainers. 'Did he come to a horrible end?' she asks.

'Very nasty,' says Flora Rose. 'You don't want to know. You'll need to push the door to make it open.'

Tilly puts one finger against the door, gives it a shove and it swings open, revealing absolute darkness. It's so black inside it feels as if the blackness is leaking out to where we're standing.

'Do you really want to go in there?' sniffs Eric.

'Ladies first,' says Jacob, shining the Dreamcaster into the void. It lights up a rickety wooden bridge, stretching over a pond.

'No, thanks,' says Tilly.

'I'll just go back to the jetty – wait for you there,' says Victor.

'Oh, no you don't!' Tilly grabs Victor's elbow. It stretches but then he comes to rest next to her. 'You're coming in with us.'

'Really?' says Victor, weakly.

'The water's called the Lilac Lake,' says Flora Rose. 'And on the other side is an island with a rose bush. The rose always blooms but the flowers are dark purple. There's a legend that the flowers bring eternal happiness. They're rather pretty actually.'

We cluster around the doorway, peering into the gloom.

'Who's going to pick me a rose then?' asks Tilly.

'I don't fancy it,' says Jacob.

'Count me out,' says Victor. 'I'll wait here. Tell you what – shall I look after your bags?'

'No thanks,' says Tilly. 'I don't trust you. Tom, pick me a rose. Go to the island and come back with a rose – a good one, not a mangy, I've-finished-flowering sort of a one. I'd like some eternal happiness please.'

'What? Why should I?' I say. 'If you want a rose you can go and pick it yourself.'

'If you don't pick one for me, I'll tell Mum AND Grandma that you were unkind.'

If I could see Tilly's face right now, I know she'd be running a mix of smug face and stuck-out lower lip.

'I'm here, Tilly, to protect you and get you out of trouble,' I say. 'I am not your servant.'

'Exactly,' she replies. 'So if you don't cross the bridge, I will, and then I'll be in trouble hanging on a broken bridge over the twin-tailed waggle fish or the man-eating piranhas, and you'll have to save me and there'll be two of us in trouble.' I can hear the smug smile in Tilly's voice. 'If you go on your own then I'm here to shout and scream and encourage you back. Or ring for an ambulance.'

I'm trying to see the world the way Tilly sees it, with her at the centre and me hanging on to some distant whim of hers, when Jacob leaps onto the first plank of the bridge. 'If you won't go, I will,' he says, striding onto the boards.

For a moment it looks as if the bridge will hold his weight, but as he takes his third stride, it lets out a yell, the plank snaps and drops him into the dark water below.

'Oh dear,' says Flora Rose. 'That is unfortunate.'

# Chapter 14

'AAAAAAArrghghghghgh!' screams Jacob, from the darkness. Splashes accompany his shouts and the angry shouts of the bridge, before coming to a gurgling halt.

A purple beam of light cuts through the water, drifting slowly down and down.

'He was still holding his torch,' says Flora Rose sadly.

Something ripples the beam and I'm sure I see a stream of bubbles rise from beneath the surface.

'Billy!' shouts Flora Rose. 'Wait!'

And another ripple shakes the weakening torch beam.

'Oh Lor, she's dived in to save him,' says Victor. 'How horribly heroic.'

We stare into the cavern, waiting for anyone or anything to resurface. It's like staring into the heart of a gigantic blackcurrant jelly baby. One that swallows things.

'Tom, save him. Save him, now,' instructs Tilly, sounding anxious.

'Can he swim?' asks Eric eventually.

'I think so,' I reply, searching my bag for anything that might help. 'Perhaps he's caught on something.' My hands close around a length of elderly rope that was being chucked out by Field Craft. It's rough and not terribly strong but it might help. I knot one end and throw it into the Lilac Lake. It falls in the light from the torch beam and slowly sinks below the surface.

'Do you think he's already dead?' asks Tilly. 'Will he come back as a ghost?'

We stare at the surface. In my head, I start to count.

*One . . .*

*Two . . .*

*Three . . .*

*Four . . .*

How long can someone hold their breath?

*Seven . . .*

*Eight . . .*

Jacob's top half shoots out of the water. 'Help!' he shouts, thrashing at the water. 'Snot Face, Model Village – get me out of here!'

'Grab the rope,' I shout. 'Right next to you.'

Spluttering, he grasps at the rope and Eric and I try to pull him out, but it snaps almost immediately, sending him back below.

'Tom, DO SOMETHING!' yells Tilly.

I'm standing there, staring, trying to work out how I can possibly rescue someone twice my size who seems to be drowning in a haunted jelly baby, when Jacob bobs back up, supported by two human shapes apparently made of purple gloop.

'You idiots!' he shouts. 'Grab some ivy or something! Shrink something, drown something! Do something! HELP ME!'

Briefly I wonder if Jacob would help any of us in the same situation, before running back out of the door and combing the ground outside the bell tower for anything useful. It's dark out here and my torch beam is feeble compared to Jacob's, and there doesn't appear to be anything much to help, and it's downright scary.

'Whhhhhhoooooooooooooo.' The distant trees let out a particularly mournful wail.

Something rustles in the undergrowth and I race back inside clutching a short stick and a couple of feeble lengths of ivy, which were the only remotely useful things I spotted. Back in the bell tower, Eric's hanging on to a rotting stump and leaning out over the water with a branch.

His branch is at least an arm too short. 'What are those things on either side of you, Jacob?' he says, stretching his hand another millimetre.

'Poor, pathetic Billy and Flora Rose,' says Victor, strolling out from the gloom. 'You can see them because of the water – it's thick and coats everything.' He turns away into the shadows and I quite clearly see a spark, the kind that comes from stone on stone. He's striking the meteorite against the walls of the tower. He's not even bothering to conceal it any more and I imagine he's trying to switch it on. I only hope I'm right about the powers not working here.

'Useless!' yells Jacob at Eric just before he sinks back under the lilac water, Flora Rose and Billy sinking with him. Although they're almost visible, Jacob is more than heavy and they're less than solid.

'They can't hold him up,' says Eric as we watch Jacob go under the water again.

'But we can't let him drown,' I say. 'We must be able to do something.'

'Why won't you work, you stupid thing?' says Victor, behind me.

We turn to look at him.

He looks up at us, caught in the beam of my torch, not unlike a fox in the headlights. 'The stick rope thingy.' He stumbles over the words. 'I was just shouting at the sticks . . .' He looks around as if noticing Jacob for the first time. 'Oh, dear, they'll never be able to hang on to him. He's so . . . large.' With an exaggerated gesture he throws himself down on the ground and crawls over the remainder of the bridge. I notice that he's not really touching the bridge, and that his grey hand now appears to be lilac – as if I'm not looking at Victor at all, but straight through to the lake.

'Hold my legs someone!' he shouts and we run to grab his ankles, Tilly too, although I don't think she's actually touching him. 'Just a little more!' shouts Victor, his hands almost closing over Jacob's before Jacob slips through his fingers and bobs back under the water.

'Oh dear – what a tragedy,' says Victor, immediately turning back towards the shore, not even stopping to watch and see if Jacob reappears for a second attempt.

'We're going to have to get that hand-tree thing,' I say to Eric.

'Really?' he says.

'Really,' I reply.

And we race out through the door, down the dark and crunchy path to the hand tree.

'Don't leave me here alone with a bunch of ghosts!' yells Tilly, charging along the path behind us.

We stop by the swamp. The tree turns a little to face us.

'It's completely horrible,' I say. 'How on earth can we get it out? Without being crushed to death?'

'As I remember, the genus *Handus* can be charmed by riddles,' says Eric. 'And jokes of course.'

'Riddles? But it hasn't even got ears!'

'Jokes and riddles? I know lots of jokes,' says Tilly. 'Doctor, doctor, I feel like a pair of curtains . . .'

To my surprise the tree seems to relax.

'Doctor doctor, I feel like a pack of cards.'

Tilly starts again. 'One night, a butcher, a baker, and a milkman enter a haunted house. Four men come out. Who is the fourth?' And the tree faces her, concentrating intently, watching her. It seems not to notice us tiptoeing across the edge of the swamp until we have our arms linked around the trunk.

'How about a limerick? *There was a boy called Tom, who ran away from a bomb. He went to a pub to get some grub . . .*'

'One, two, three – lift!' I hiss, and Eric and I pull, ignoring the awful squelching sound around our feet. The roots, although wide, aren't particularly long, and after three goes we actually get it out of the ground.

'Quick, we'd better run back,' says Eric, and between the three of us we try to pull it along the path. The arms are still flailing but so long as Tilly tells it riddles, it seems less aggressive, if a tree can seem less aggressive.

'I'm here, I'm here!' shouts a voice from the mist.

'Victor?' asks Eric.

'Yes, yes, can't let the poor mite drown. Hand tree eh? Very resourceful – let me help.'

Between the four of us we get back to the shore of the lake, just in time to see Jacob's limp hand sink below the surface.

'Now!'

We shove the tree out over the water, and without Tilly's riddles, it twists around searching for something to grab. Finding Jacob, it plucks him from the water, drags him towards the shore accompanied by his two strange jelly-ghost floats and holds him high in the air.

'Bravo!' says Eric.

'Result,' coughs Jacob, throwing up a week's worth of sweets.

'How very . . . necessary,' says Victor.

# Chapter 15

The tree really likes Jacob. It won't let him go even with Tilly standing there telling it riddles and laughing at her own jokes.

'Help! Help!' Jacob shouts, caught struggling in the branches like a huge purple beetle in a spider's web.

I'm so out of breath I can only stand and stare and gulp air.

'Oh for goodness' sake,' says Tilly. She pokes the tree in the joints between the branches and the trunk. 'Let go of him,' she orders in her best dog-trainer voice.

The tree squeaks, releases Jacob and rolls its branches over the trunk protectively, as if Tilly had actually tickled it in its armpits.

The moment it does, we rush out of the bell tower, abandoning the flailing tree on the side of the Lilac Lake.

I glance back at the writhing branches dripping purple liquid onto the floor, and shudder. I almost feel sorry for it – and then I remember Vile Lucy and catch up with the others.

'So how are we going to get home?' I ask as we stumble back in the half-light towards the broken harbour. 'The boat's not due back for hours. I mean, Tilly, you dragged us here – you must have had a plan.'

We stop in the graveyard next to the harbour.

Tilly flicks her hair over her shoulder. 'Plan? I thought you had a plan, Tom. You were here to look after me. I assumed you'd thought about it.'

I decide not to answer her. Beside her are what must be Flora Rose and Billy. They're almost visible as a result of the lilac goo. Billy's quite little, wearing a cap, a waistcoat and long shorts like a Victorian chimney boy. I can't really see his features, but Flora Rose is clearer – she's bent over, studying the shiny buckles on Tilly's handbag. I imagine she's looking at herself, and I can see that she isn't all that old, maybe 12 or 162 if I add in the extra 150 years. They're like a pair of black-and-white photos tinted purple, and a touch see-through.

Weird, and a little sad.

'Maybe there's an airship or something here,' says Tilly. 'Didn't the Victorians have airships? Tom, you could talk a lot and fill it with hot air.' She smiles sweetly and drains my water bottle.

'My dear child, there are NO airships here,' says Victor, sighing and standing close to Jacob who is removing large clods of purple jelly from his clothing.

'This stuff is really sticky,' says Jacob.

'Come to the sea, dear boy. Let's see if we can wash it off,' says Victor.

I watch them go, wondering if I need to follow. But they can't get off the island – no one can unless we build a boat or wait for the

*Trusty Mermaid* – so I let Victor take Jacob out of sight. After all, there's only so much of Jacob that anyone can stand.

'Let's face it. We're going to have to build a raft,' says Eric.

'How?' asks Tilly. 'Don't you need tree trunks and rope and things?'

I pull open the graveyard-shed door, which comes away in my hand. There's a heap of rotting rubbish on one side, a sled, a couple of rusty buckets, a rotting boat and an axe. I pick up the axe and to my surprise the handle feels quite solid.

Underneath that I find a saw. Blunt, but still a saw.

'Right, if we're going to build a raft, we need loads of wood.'

'The Fearful Forest?' says Eric. 'It is trees after all.'

I stand on the edge of the graveyard looking towards the sea. There's more light out there. The centre of the island looks completely black, not at all inviting. That forest is at least ten minutes' walk into the gloom.

'That forest'll have to go,' I say in a voice that sounds an awful lot more confident than I feel. 'As you say, they're only trees.' I swing the axe over my shoulder. 'Anyone coming with me? Anyone going to help?'

'I'm staying here,' says Tilly, pulling two soggy Woodland Friends from her bag and arranging them on a gravestone. 'Call me when you've finished.'

'I'll come,' says Eric, picking up the saw. 'Jacob?' he calls towards the harbour.

'Leave him, I say – he's covered in purple stuff.'

'Flora Rose?' I ask. Two purple blobs emerge from the shadows at the far side of the graveyard. 'Can you guide us to the Fearful Forest?'

'If you're sure,' says Flora Rose, sighing. 'You might want to stuff your ears with something – it gets louder the closer you get. I'll just go and tell the other two what we're doing.'

'Shall we sing to keep off the creeps?' says Eric, picking up bundles of black moss from the ground and handing me half. I try to turn it into earplugs but it crumbles and falls out, leaving me with gritty ears. Eric marches into the darkness and launches into the Field Craft Troop anthem, 'We Are Hardly Scared of Anything'.

'We are hardly scared of anything,
We can barely fear the raven's wing,
But bold be our stride with our cut staff at
    our side . . .'

Our walking slows a touch as unseen things grab at our arms, but I keep pressing forward and we plunge into verse two.

'We are hardly scared of anything . . .'

'What an awful song,' says Flora Rose, appearing at my elbow. 'I think we should go back to the harbour – have you ever heard of the SS *Devlin*?'
    'Jacob's dad's boat? Why?'
    'I think they've called Jacob's father on the mobile communication machine. He's coming to get them. Him and Victor.'
    'Do you mean – not us? Not the rest of us?'

Both Flora Rose and Billy nod their heads vigorously.

'I'm struggling to understand this,' says Eric.

I'm about to ask her how she knows when Tilly screams behind us. 'But you can't do that – you can't just abandon us!'

I turn to listen, staring with horror at Eric's shocked face staring back at me.

'You beast, Jacob Devlin! I'll get you for that! I'll never forget – Tilly Perks never forgets!'

There's the distant sound of a motorboat.

'YOU RAT! YOU COMPLETE SEWER RAT! How could you do THIS to ME!' Tilly's voice slides from angry to tears.

'Oh dear,' says Flora Rose. 'I think we may be slightly too late.'

# Chapter 16

'They've gone!' shouts Tilly, crashing back along the track, ignoring the ghastly sound of screaming trees as my axe bites into the first trunk. 'Jacob's left us here! It's outrageous!'

'So is this Victor's work?' asks Eric, pulling on a branch which springs back, thwacking him in the face. 'Ow!' he protests and rubs his nose.

The purple figure that must be Billy scrapes a YES on a nearby rock.

'I knew it,' I say.

'What?' says Tilly.

'That Victor was trouble. I could see it from the moment we found him.'

'Well, why didn't you tell me?' says Tilly, flaring her nostrils and doing a passable impression of a hayfevered horse before stopping to wipe something from her shoe.

I ignore her.

'Well, I'm cross,' says Eric. 'Really, quite cross.' He shakes his head and his curls flop over his face. 'I feel let down. Yes, that's it. Betrayed.' He holds his finger up, making a point. 'Betrayed by both of them. Victor said he could help – and we've just rescued Jacob.' He kicks the ground. 'Actually, I feel foolish. Taken in. An absolute mug.'

Flora Rose sighs. 'Victor isn't terribly nice, actually.' She smiles, and the lilac water over her face smiles too. 'In fact, he's pretty beastly.' She wanders over to a pool of black, brackish water and gazes at her purple reflection.

'So when you say that – do you mean that we should be worrying about what happens to Jacob?' I ask.

'Well . . .' She swishes her ghostly skirt back and

forth, and pulls an angry face at her reflection. 'He's clever, he's selfish, and he's greedy. Does that answer your question?'

'What's he greedy for?' I ask, managing to slice through the first tree trunk after hitting it about a billion times.

'POWER,' Billy scratches in the sand at our feet.

'Power?' I say, watching a white balloon-shaped thing rise from the timber and float into the sky.

'That's one of the spirits,' says Flora Rose. 'You've actually managed to release one – brilliant. Anyway . . .' She tears herself away from the pool. 'I think he wants your powers. I know it sounds silly but it's so that he can take over the world. He loves what Jacob can do with the sparks.'

'Take over the world?' says Tilly, panting to a halt next to Flora Rose. 'Who wants to take over the world?'

'Victor,' says Eric, wrinkling his face in pain. 'Oh dear. We had better do something. We can't just leave Jacob with a power-hungry ghoul. We are supposed to be his friends.'

He doesn't look convinced.

'Well, you'd better hurry up then, Tom,' says Tilly, sitting down on the felled tree trunk. 'And if I was you I'd catch him and stick him right back in that purple swamp.'

'He did leave us here,' I say.

'We don't need to rush,' says Eric.

'No,' I say, starting on the next tree trunk. My axe bounces off the wood leaving it untouched. 'But at this rate it could be days before we manage to build a raft. Look at how long it's taking me.'

Tilly and Eric pitch in, and between us we fell four screaming trees and free four screaming spirits. The whole thing makes me shudder, but once we have the four trunks, they are just like four normal tree trunks. We roll them down to the shore, where it's light.

'We're going to have to get a move on,' I say. 'They'll be back at home by now, and who knows what Victor can get Jacob to do for him? He stole Jacob's meteorite by the way.'

'*Mine* and Jacob's if you don't mind. But our

powers only work in Bywater-by-Sea,' says Eric, as if it's only just occurred to him. 'You can't really do anything special outside the village. That's why we can't use them here. And you have to find a meteorite just after it's fallen to get any power in the first place. I mean, it's all very well, but anything Victor thinks he can do, he can only do in the village. And he can't actually do anything anyway, because he hasn't caught a meteorite.'

I close my eyes, trying to make sense of what Eric just said.

'Really?' says Flora Rose, trying and failing to stop one of the trunks rolling away.

'He's right about the meteorites,' I say, lugging the trunk back up the slope. 'But, Eric, the castle dust is different. It can make strange things happen. I know it's firmly locked up, but sooner or later he's going to work out how to get into that cell, and then what's going to happen?'

'Is that what made him human?' asks Flora Rose.

'Yes, almost certainly,' says Eric. 'And it must

have washed off when we all got tipped in the sea. It doesn't work outside Bywater-by-Sea either. But inside the village it can cause huge disruption.'

'But don't forget,' I say, 'Victor is a ghost – we have no idea what the dust would do for him. It might work outside the village. It could work anywhere in the world. He might actually be able to do extraordinary things.'

'Do you think he'd actually harm Jacob?' Eric asks Flora Rose.

A purple Y appears on a blank stone at my feet. Followed by an E and S.

Flora Rose shrugs. 'I think Billy's right. Victor's capable of anything.'

'Right,' I say. 'Let's get this thing finished at full speed – we HAVE to rescue Jacob, whether or not he deserves it. And we have to stop Victor.'

The raft is lumpy. It's not watertight and it turns out that it's impossible to steer.

'Try pushing again,' says Eric, watching the tiny gap between us and the crumbling jetty get even smaller. 'I'm sure if we can get out into the open sea it'll be easier to get some forward motion.'

'It's raining,' says Tilly, helpfully.

'I know,' I say, 'and I'm trying as hard as possible but it's just not easy. You could help, you know.'

Tilly suddenly finds something in her bag really interesting.

'If I just . . .' Eric wedges a long tree branch in the gap and puts his weight on it, pushing us away from the jetty until we begin to drift out through the fog and there's a tantalising glimpse of the open sea. 'Give me a lever long enough and I will move the world,' he says, frantically dabbing with his branch to increase our speed.

'Eh?' I say, paddling with a section of shed door on the other side of the boat.

'Archimedes,' he says. '*Give me a lever long enough and a pivot on which to place it and I will move the world.* δῶς μοι πᾶ στῶ καὶ τὰν γᾶν κινάσω. It's Greek, you know.'

'Ah,' I say. 'Of course.'

We splash at the water, slowly finding a rhythm, until we're deep in the mist, a fine drizzle coating Eric's glasses.

'You're doing frightfully well,' says a voice above us in the fog.

'Flora Rose,' says Eric. 'Are you coming with us?'

'Naturally,' she says. 'We can't leave you without help – and anyway, who'd want to stay there on the island when there's so much fun and warmth on the mainland?'

There's almost silence as our makeshift oars plip in the sea, moving us forward little by little.

'Victor wouldn't have helped you rescue Jacob, you know. He was just trying to get that rock to do its thing.'

'Why'd you say that?' I ask.

'Because,' says Flora Rose, 'I just wanted you to know what he's really like. He'd have let Jacob drown.'

'So what changed his mind?' I ask.

'I reminded him . . .' She pauses. 'That Jacob's the one with the spark.'

'What?' says Tilly. 'Are you saying I'm boring?'

'No,' says Flora Rose. 'I don't mean that. I mean, he gives off sparks and that's the thing that Victor wants. He's never seen the rest of you do anything – well, anything useful – except for the inflatable oar this morning.'

'Is Billy there with you?' asks Eric, staring vaguely upwards.

'Oh yes, he's the one who insisted we come. He's really very sweet – such a shame you can't hear what he says.'

'Surely you could just fly over? Couldn't you?' asks Tilly, dangling her fingers in the water alongside the raft.

'Not really,' says Flora Rose. 'We need something to hang on to. We might just blow away if there wasn't something solid nearby.'

'Interesting,' says Eric. 'You need a corporeal mass for anchorage.'

No one quite knows how to reply so we struggle on through the mist in more silence.


It's raining hard now, possibly getting dark, and I'm completely tired with the rowing lark.

'Tom,' says Tilly, creeping across the raft. 'I'm scared.'

'Don't be,' says Flora Rose. 'I can see the harbour.'

'Really?' Tilly stands up, rocking the raft until I nearly drop my piece of shed-door oar in the sea. 'Where? Where? Hurry up you useless pair! We could be home in time for lunch.'

'Well, more like tea,' says Flora Rose. 'It's quite a long way, and I'm quite high up.'

'Yes – triangulation can give a deceptive sense of distance,' says Eric from the darkness on the other side of the raft.

'But it's so wet,' moans Tilly. 'I don't like it.'

Slowly, above our heads, something like a huge jellyfish appears, glowing against the thunderous sky.

'Oh Billy, how sweet,' says Flora Rose.

The sky jellyfish wriggles and bounces and I see that it's surrounded by the faint purple outline of a boy.

It is comforting, if completely useless as an umbrella.

# Chapter 17

'So you're not going to help then?' I call after Tilly as she marches up the hill from the harbour.

'Certainly not,' she says without even turning to look. 'It's all your fault, Tom – everything about everything is your fault.'

Eric stares at her back, disappearing amongst the afternoon day trippers. 'I'm quite glad I don't have a sister.'

I don't say anything. I expect that if Eric had a sister she'd be as clever as he is and I'd have two of them telling me how things work and that would be intolerable – especially if you added in Jacob and Tilly as well.

We lug the raft onto the beach. It looks ordinary – if really badly made. No one would know that the planks had once held spirits. Now they just seem to hold huge amounts of seawater.

'We need to find Jacob and Victor,' says Eric as I squeeze water from my socks.

'As soon as possible,' says Flora Rose from right behind me.

In the afternoon light, Flora Rose and Billy are barely visible. A couple of purple smudges move at the edge of my vision, but if I look at them, I can't really see them. It would be easy to forget that they were there.

'Where do you suppose they are?' I ask.

'Victor will want to get back into the castle . . .' starts Flora Rose.

'But Jacob will want to eat something . . .' I make myself hungry thinking about this morning's chips.

'Hm,' Eric interrupts me. 'You have a point. But –'

'There!' shouts Flora Rose. 'There they are, by the castle.'

I swing round, possibly passing right through Billy but trying not to think about it, and look up at the castle. Strolling down the hill are Victor and Jacob. Victor is still hazy. He's obviously trying to look like a casual tourist, a borrowed straw hat on his head and what looks like a borrowed pair of Jacob's dad's shorts on his grey legs. In between, his long coat, tie and high-collared grimy shirt just make him look like a complete madman. One that's lost his trousers and tried to find a substitute at a jumble sale.

'Gosh,' says Eric.

'Shh,' I say, ducking my head below the sea wall. 'I think we'd better follow.'

They take the long way down; we take the short cut and slip into the tunnel where we first saw the ghosts. Eric and I back into a dripping doorway. I try the door behind us and it opens but we can't get inside because it's full of hundreds of cartons of cocoa powder.

'We'll just have to make do with the doorway,' says Eric.

We step back out and put our backs against the wooden door and in the gloom Flora Rose and Billy disappear completely.

'What are we waiting for?' says Flora Rose from disturbingly close.

'We're waiting for –'

'Shh,' I say, as footsteps sound in the corridors.

'Bet you wish you were still a proper ghost,' Jacob's voice echoes cheerily from the stones. 'You could have slipped in and helped yourself.' I shrink back against the wall as Jacob stops outside the end cell, the one piled high with pots of the dust that come from the mine that Professor Lee dug. Like all the others, it's firmly locked.

Victor stares longingly through the bars.

'Won't you help me?' says Victor, gently. 'I mean, from what you say, this, in addition to your . . . remarkable power, would make us invincible. We could do anything, and who could stop us?'

'Tempting,' says Jacob. 'But not that tempting. I'm the most powerful person in the town just at the moment – I don't think I want to change that. Now I think it's time we investigated the tea shop. They do a lovely chocolate cake.'

'Perhaps you could get me just enough to stop me fading in and out? Just a little?' Victor stretches his arms past the bars, but even though he's half ghost, he's not ghostly enough to get through and, as a half human, he's not going to be able to reach anything. 'No, sorreeee. Not going to,' says Jacob, swinging back up the corridor. 'C'mon upstairs to the tea shop. We need to get a table before all the day trippers turn up.'

I send up thanks for Jacob's selfishness. He could easily melt the bars, even with the danger that stray sparks could ignite the dust inside the cell.

'Blast. Drat and blast,' says Victor, sighing, and he follows Jacob up the stairs towards the castle café.

'So he does want the dust,' says Eric. 'But he can't get it, not unless he gets the key to the cell – and he won't, will he, Tom? I mean, your grandma's got one but apart from that, who else?'

I shrug, imagining the key to the cell hanging

in the key cabinet at home – marked *END CELL CASTLE DUNGEON* in Grandma's careful capitals.

'He'll find a way,' says Flora. 'He'll either find the key, or charm the key from your grandmother, Tom, or he'll find a way in without it. He's waited a hundred and fifty years for this. He's going to get what he wants.'

'Not,' I say, 'if we stop him first.'

# Chapter 18

'Oooh,' whispers Flora Rose in my ear. 'What pretty curtains. Is this what people do for fun? I like it.'

'Shh,' I say, searching the castle café for Jacob and Victor. It's difficult to see anyone – the place is so busy and so full of flowers and flowery wallpaper.

Eric nudges me, pointing to a table against the window. On the top perches a huge cake stand, piled high with cupcakes, waffles and scones. Squeezed into the tiny amount of remaining space is a bottle of Go-Stiser fizz, a can of Verucazade and, seated on either side, Victor and Jacob.

'So, anyway, I thought we could do a round of crazy golf next . . .' Jacob's voice rings through the tea shop.

'You go and play golf, dear fellow. I'm happy here. I can sit in the sun outside the castle and wait for you,' says Victor, sniffing at a waffle in interest. 'Are these curious things pleasant?'

'D'ishous,' mumbles Jacob around a mouthful of cake. 'And you should try this.' He holds up the can of Verucazade.

We take a table with three chairs at the side, sitting so that we can see what's going on at Jacob's table. The third chair trembles slightly as Flora Rose sits down.

'We need to get them apart. We need to talk to Jacob alone,' says Eric, holding up the menu to hide his face, but completely failing to conceal his wild ginger hair. 'We're going to need him for our plan to work.'

'I could just shrink Victor,' I say.

'What, here? In a tea room?' says Eric. 'Your grandma would be furious.'

'Shall I whisper to Jacob?' says Flora Rose. 'Tell him the truth about Victor?' The purple goo's gone completely and now she's just an alarming voice from nowhere.

'Victor would hear,' I say.

'You could, Billy, but how?' says Flora Rose. The silver sugar bowl on the table shows the faintest purple reflection.

'What's he saying?' asks Eric.

'He says he could give Jacob a message.'

'What? Write it in crumbs or something?' I say.

The vase of flowers in the middle of the table trembles in answer.

'Well,' I say. 'OK, if you really think it'll work.'

We watch as Jacob ignores all Billy's attempts to rearrange the cake crumbs. He brushes at the air as if there's a fly buzzing around him. 'Thing about golf is, it doesn't really require any effort – go away, thing!' He flaps the cake stand with the back of his hand, sending cupcakes cascading across the café.

One rolls and stops at my foot. I look up across the room and catch Jacob's gaze.

His eyes open wide in recognition and he raises

his arm to point at me, but I mime a mouth zip and, frowning, Jacob says nothing. I glance at Victor, but he's chewing a waffle and looking at something he obviously finds really interesting outside the window.

'Would you like to order?' says a jolly waitress, bowling up to our table.

'Could we just have –' starts Eric.

'Could we choose from the cakes on the side?' I interrupt, smiling and hoping very much that Eric's got some money because I've got barely anything.

'Of course,' says the waitress. 'You have a good look and tell me what you fancy.'

'Why are we doing this?' whispers Eric, rising from the table and trailing over to the large table of cakes. 'It's going to cost a fortune.'

'We're giving Jacob a message ourselves.'

I point to the signs on the cakes, widening my eyes and pointing again until Jacob's paying proper attention.

'*Custard pie, blackcurrant crumble cake?*' he reads aloud, peering across the café at the cake table.

I shake my head and nod towards Victor, who is still staring out of the window.

'*Pineapple surprise, Victoria sponge, maids of honour* . . . No – no maids of honour, *devils on horseback*.' Jacob wrinkles his nose in incomprehension.

Eric nods, measuring a short piece of air to indicate that Jacob should make the words smaller.

'*Pineapple, sponge, maids, horseback?*'

I shake my head vigorously as the waitress piles our plates high with food, mixing sausages and cakes. I point at the labels and mouth, 'Try again.'

Like the sun coming out after heavy rain, a look of intelligence crosses Jacob's face. 'Oh, I get it.'

'What do you get?' says Victor, a slight smile crossing his face. 'Anyway, lovely tea – thank you, Jacob. I think I'll just nip out and get some air.' He springs to his feet, takes another glance out of the window and heads out of the main entrance of the tea shop, the one that leads to the castle courtyard.

'Right,' says Jacob, his head nodding slowly. '*Surprise, Victoria, no honour, devil*. Yes, Victor, I'll join you in a moment. I just need to sort out one or two things.'

# Chapter 19

'Well, it's just that we need to get rid of the dust,' says Eric for the third time to Jacob.

'But I don't understand why?'

'To stop Victor!'

'But why would we want to stop Victor? He's the most interesting thing to happen to Bywater-by-Sea forever – and why do you think he's bad? I haven't once seen him stick his finger up his nose. Everyone knows that evil people stick their fingers up their noses.'

I leave Eric shaking his head and arranging cakes on the table to illustrate the plan, and race out of the café into the passage that leads to the courtyard.

'So you think that between you, you can carry Grandma's key here to me?'

'Totally,' says Flora Rose's voice from nowhere. 'It's in the key cupboard, big label, huge piece of string. Billy and I'll be fine. And we'll be back in seconds. We can go so much faster than you can.'

'Go carefully,' I say, and, for a moment, the sunlight of the courtyard is dimmed by the two spirits racing out of the passage. I almost see them, and then I spot Victor.

He's hiding behind the bins, watching the workmen cutting out an old metal drain cover in the middle of the courtyard. Eventually, the workmen wander off into the shade to eat their lunch, leaving their tools in a heap by the wall.

For a long time nothing moves except a crow. It flies down, pecks at the ground and takes a long slow look at Victor.

It hops towards him and stops by the bins, its head tilted to one side, watching.

I see Victor flap his hands at it, obviously trying to frighten it away, but the bird takes it as encouragement and hops a little closer, its black shiny eye fixed on Victor's furious face.

'Buzz off,' he says, waving his arms, but the bird leans forward and pecks at his outstretched hand.

Flora Rose's voice sounds in my ear. 'Here,' she says and right in front of my nose hangs Grandma's key.

'Brilliant,' I whisper. 'Can you take it to Eric? He and Jacob know what to do. I'm going to keep an eye on Victor.'

The key floats off down the passage. I only hope they don't give some passing tourist a heart attack.

I go back to watching Victor and the crow. Distantly, in the castle dungeon, I hear a series of booms and a light sprinkling of glitter falls on the courtyard. Good – they're destroying the dust.

I'm sure Eric knows exactly what he's doing and Jacob doesn't need much encouragement to blow things up, but I'm sorry to have missed the fireworks display.

'Oh honestly,' says Victor, standing up and trying to look as if everyone always hides behind the bins talking to crows.

I stay in my hiding place and watch as he ambles over to the wall and pretends to look up at the tower above. There's no one there to see and nothing to look at. He looks up at nothing for about two minutes and then swoops backwards towards the workmen's tools.

It takes him a millisecond to steal the oxyacetylene torch and the cylinder. It's obviously very heavy so his progress across the courtyard is slow, but now I know what he has in mind, I race straight back through the tea shop, down the steps and reach the cell.

It's perfect. It looks exactly as it did before, except that there's a large pile of dust right in the middle of the room. It's slightly glittery, as it should be, and there's an almost imperceptible smell of burned chocolate powder.

There's no sign of Eric and Jacob.

'Flora Rose?' I say into the air.

Nothing.

'Billy?'

A sudden wind falls on my cheek and I have the odd sensation that I'm standing in a corridor with a spirit that I can't see or hear, but I know he's there.

'Here, Tom.' The tiny voice springs out next to my elbow. It's not Flora Rose.

'Billy?' I say, trying not to shiver. 'Is that you?'

'Me,' he says. 'Just me.'

'How amazing to meet you,' I say, and I throw a handful of dust up in the air. It drapes itself over a shape in the middle of the space, and I see a glimmer of a little boy with a hat and shorts and a mushroom sort of a nose.

But he doesn't manage to speak again.

'Good,' I say. I can't think of anything else to say. A breath of wind falls on my cheek and a cold finger brushes over my palm.

Footsteps sound at the top of the passage to the courtyard, accompanied by the uncomfortable screech of a heavy, metal gas tank being dragged over flagstones.

A minute or two later and Victor appears, struggling and cursing. 'Cretinous invention, impossibly unintelligent way to get through anything. Strewth but it's so heavy!' The cylinder breaks free and rolls down the passage, clanging into the bars of the cell, and bowling Victor over like a skittle.

'Ow! Blasted thing.' He scrambles to his feet, dragging the rest of the torch over the cobbles and then stopping outside the cell. 'Oh yes,' he says, gazing at the piles and pots of dust inside. 'Oh yes – wonderful new world of shining sparkling things, you are so nearly mine.'

He stands, holding the tube and torch in one hand and the top of the gas bottle with the other.

'So how do you two make friends then?' he asks. 'Do you go in there? Or do you go in there?'

I realise that as a Victorian he might never have seen an oxyacetylene torch and that there's a distant chance he might not be able to make the two things go together, but no such luck, as it only takes him a couple of minutes to not only get it linked but also to get it fired up.

'Oh la!' he says as the huge flame leaps from the torch and then focuses into something tiny and bright. 'Now, you tiny little self-important bits of metal – feel my rage.'

The bars fall away from the flame like sticks of butter and within a minute he has cut a doorway and is standing inside the cell, pots and pots of dust arranged around him.

I panic.

Supposing Flora Rose and Billy dropped the key on their way back to Eric and Jacob? Supposing they haven't changed the dust for chocolate powder – supposing I've just failed to prevent him from being the most powerful evil genius in the world?

He empties a pot of dust over his head and begins to laugh. The dust flies up into the air around him, glittering and spinning in the draught. 'I have it! I have it! This is it! I am invincible, unstoppable! Fire and water, come to me, make me strong!'

He dances, he whirls, he laughs, he shouts, and I'm more and more worried. He appears to be becoming more solid, less grey, but it's difficult to tell in the dull red glow of the bulb. It could just be that he's getting coated in chocolate, or it could be that there's still some magic dust left in there. 'Yes, yes, yes! At last. Bow down, World, before me. I am the most powerful being of all time, the greatest man alive, or dead. Everything shall be mine – all mine,' and he giggles madly, tasting the dust on his tongue, rubbing it into his hair, his hands, his clothes. He pauses and licks his hand. 'Mmmm, chocolate! Oh wonderful dust, you taste of chocolate. How appropriate! AWE-SOME! I am a god, a demigod, an all-things god, a superpower. I am that rare thing, a superhero with a brain – they will worship me!'

He's reached the stage of lying on the floor on his back like a dog, chucking handfuls of dust into the air, when quite suddenly the ground gives way beneath him.

It's my cue and I race out and up the passage, out of the castle courtyard and around the outside of the walls, tumbling and tripping over the tussocks and earthworks until I see Eric and

Jacob standing staring at the bottom of the ancient medieval toilet chute.

Finding an extra burst of energy in my legs I race over the grass to join them.

'Wow!' says Eric.

'Awesome!' says Jacob.

An explosion of chocolate powder bursts from the wall – followed by a heavy thump.

There on the ground in front of us is Victor, pale and chocolatey in uneven patches. He gazes at his hand. Beneath the cocoa powder it's definitely faded to grey. 'Oh no,' he says. 'I'm turning back into a ghost. This is terri—' But before he's finished speaking, Eric turns on the sprinklers at the end of his fingers and drenches him with freezing cold water, washing off all the castle's magic dust and all the chocolate powder.

'Chaps!' he manages to stutter. I form my thumb and forefinger into an O, step back so that Victor is right in the middle and . . .

Click.

# Chapter 20

'Chaps - this is not fair!' Victor squeaks. 'Not fair at all.'

'Now what?' asks Jacob, crouching down to look at the curious little grey figure squirming in the puddle. 'Did I look like this when you shrank me?'

'Yes, kind of, but redder and . . . rounder,' I say, taking a small, yellow, plastic capsule out of my pocket. 'Let's put him in here for now.'

'He'll suffocate in there,' says Eric.

'He's only half human,' I say.

'Exactly,' says Flora Rose from nowhere. 'The minute he gets more ghostly he'll be out of there.

You can't imprison ghosts. And you won't be able to see him.'

We stumble down the long grass slope until we reach the path that winds up the hill towards the model village.

'Couldn't we keep him underwater?' asks Jacob, panting along at the back.

'What about a metal box? A lead box?' says Eric. 'Even radiation can't get through that.'

'No, it won't work – we can go through anything. We can fly, float. We're indestructible,' says Flora Rose from above.

Jacob screws up his face in thought. 'How do you get to be a ghost?' he asks.

Sometimes the depths of Jacob's lack of intelligence astonish me.

'So what do we do with him?' asks Eric. 'We can't let him go – he's dangerous.'

He holds open the gate at the bottom of the model village and we pass through. I look at the capsule in my hand. I hope Victor's still in there – I wouldn't want him to fall out here and haunt the model village. That would go down really badly with Grandma.

'Yes,' says Flora Rose. 'Billy, you're right.'

'What did Billy say?' I ask.

'He says you're going to have to offer Victor something he really wants. You've got to make it worth his while to stay away. In fact, you're going to have to bribe him. There's no point in appealing to his better nature – he hasn't got one.'

We wander up to the house and I push open the front door. There's no sign of Grandma so we pile into the kitchen and settle on both sides of the table. Actually, there's only me and Eric and Jacob – the other two are completely invisible. You could almost imagine they didn't exist.

I take a jam jar from the window sill and open the yellow pod. Victor's still visible, slumped on the bottom, his head resting on his hands.

'Oh, it's you,' he says dismally and goes on staring at the plastic walls.

Gently, although I'd love to be more enthusiastic, I pour Victor from one container to the other.

'He needs some food in there.' Jacob snaps off a piece of exploding chocolate volcano and drops it into the jar. It immediately pops, chasing

Victor round and round the bottom of the jar in a random series of tiny explosions.

'Oops,' says Jacob, reaching back inside the jar to get it out.

Victor cowers at the bottom, his hands over his head. 'Leave me alone,' he wails. 'I never did anyone any harm. I'm an innocent creature – honestly, believe me.'

'Don't,' says Flora Rose. 'Don't believe him. He's lying.'

Eric balances a copy of *1,000 Quite Difficult Recipes for Tea Shops* on top of the jar and we stare through the glass.

Victor's almost invisible.

'Flora Rose is right. Given another twelve hours we won't be able to keep him,' says Eric, 'unless we expose him to dust, and if we expose him to dust who knows what powers he'll develop.' He heaves a long sigh and I think back to what Billy said.

'You need, says Billy, to improve the island,' says Flora Rose. 'So that it's a home rather than a prison.'

'Really?' says Jacob. 'Like a makeover?'

Eric nods wisely.

'So if we improve the island, what do you all want?' I ask wearily, my hand poised over a sheet of paper with a stump of Grandma's shopping-list pencil. 'I mean, bearing in mind we're only human.'

'Billy wants friends,' says Flora Rose. 'He wants people to come. Children to play with. He's only little, and I must say, it gets pretty dull talking to skeletons all the time. I'd like some nice people, day trippers who go away at night. I'd like street lights, someone to remove all the rotting houses where the ghouls hang out. I'd like cheerful gardens, a vegetable patch, an orchard, and tea shops like you have here, with pretty wallpaper, and a house of my own with soft beds and nice clean sheets. I'd like . . .'

'You can't even lie in a bed, you stupid creature. You're a ghost!' squeaks Victor from his jam-jar prison.

Something brushes against my leg. 'Yow! What was that?'

'Shipwreck James,' says Flora Rose. 'OOOOWWWW, you lovely creature, come to

Mummy, oh yes, cuddles, and boojiboojiboojums, yes, yes . . .'

I find myself shuddering, not sure whether it's the overload of cat love or the idea of a ghost girl and a ghost cat having a mutual love-in which we can hear but can't see.

'Oh do shut up, Flora Rose,' moans Victor.

'OH!!!! Was that Victor talking? Tom! You shrank him, how perfect. He's so cuuuuuute!' says Tilly, wandering into the kitchen. 'Can I have him? Keep him with the Woodland Friends? Please Tom, please?'

'No!' I echo with Victor.

'You're no fun,' says Tilly. 'You've finally shrunk someone worth having and you won't let me have him.'

'He's a dangerous lunatic,' says Flora Rose. 'Believe me, you don't want him. You'd lose all your little furry creatures within days. He'd do something horrible to them.'

'Like, dismember them? Cool,' says Tilly. 'Please, Tom.'

'No,' I say. 'And that's final.'

'He'll grow back anyway,' says Eric. 'You'd only have him small for a few days.'

Tilly leaves the kitchen, slamming the door behind her. She stamps her way up the stairs and into her bedroom, making absolutely everything vibrate so that a swathe of cobwebs that have so far clung to the ceiling over the stove float gently to the floor, releasing a cloud of dead flies.

'And what do *you* want, Victor?' asks Eric, staring hard at a shadow caught in the cobwebs that might possibly be Flora Rose, or Billy.

'Power, I just want power,' Victor says. 'But it's all been ruinnnned.' He sinks to the bottom of the jam jar and hides his head in his hands.

'Like electricity?' says Jacob.

'Well, apart from power, what would you like? What would keep you on the island?' I ask.

'I want a castle,' Victor mutters. 'And I do want electricity, and light, and comfort, and one of those screen things with a shooty thing and controls.'

'He means a games console,' says Jacob. 'He's got his priorities right.'

'But there is no electricity on the island,' says Eric. 'It's four miles off shore – no one's ever put so much as a single lighthouse on it.'

'Well, you're going to have to solve it, or I won't go away. I will stay here forever and ever and make everyone do what I want one way or another. I will make your lives a misery.'

'OK,' I say.

'That's too much. Ridiculous. You'd need to spend thousands,' says Eric. 'Maybe millions. We can't possibly do that. We can't possibly do any of it. It's all utterly unrealistic. It's as mad as trying to move the bird sanctuary – it just can't be done. And while we're thinking of you, Victor, can we have our meteorite back, please?'

'Oh honestly,' squeaks Victor, and I hear the ping of the meteorite clattering down the wall of the jam jar. Outside the kitchen window Grandma's in full swing painting her placards that are arranged around the garden: *Turn back for the Little Tern. Roller coasters are not fun for everyone.* And other snappy slogans.

'So you would actually like Mystery Smoke Island developed.'

'Yes,' say Flora Rose and Victor.

'Who on earth would want to do that?' says Eric, flicking a stray piece of volcano chocolate back up into the air and down into the jam jar.

Victor hides his head in his hands as the popping candy explodes.

I stare into the jar, imagining something mad – something totally crazy and brilliant.

'I've an idea – but I need to talk to Grandma.'

'What?' says Eric.

'I'm still working it out,' I say. 'But when I've solved it, you'll be the absolute first to know, I promise.'


'Tom,' says Grandma, placing her rubber-gloved hands on either side of my head and jerking me forwards so that the inevitable kiss lands somewhere between my hair and my nose, 'I'm so proud – what a fantastic solution. But I'm not going to come with you. You'll have to work it out on your own.'

'Oh, Grandma!'

'It'll be so much better coming from you. I'm

just an old battleaxe on a bandwagon. They're sick to the back teeth of me – and the Worthies. They want someone different, and your idea's brilliant.'

'Really?'

'Yes, go on. The mayor's all right really, even if he is a money-grasping so and so.'

I turn to run and then remember something. 'Grandma, you know when you told me about ghosts being unpredictable. How did you know? Has this happened before?'

'Oh – well, only sort of. Years ago one Halloween, a couple of drunken ghosts blew over to the mainland. They caused the most awful chaos – salt in the milk, holes in boats, fish in the water tanks, that sort of thing. There was an old woman who could see them. She took them back to the island. I imagine when they sobered up they had no idea what had happened.'

'So who was she?'

'Your great-grandmother, Tom. Now get on with it, before the bulldozers move in.'

# Chapter 21

Grandma keeps everything. Cardboard, tinfoil, chocolate boxes, plastic things in the exact shape of a banana – and she keeps them all in the shed in the garden.

'Take anything, build it here,' she says, sweeping a city of paint pots to one side.

I gaze at the huge pile of recycling and try really hard to believe that we can build something fantastic.

'So – we need a roller coaster for a start.' Jacob picks up a shoebox and cuts it in half. It looks like a shoebox cut in half.

'And a ghost train,' he says, plonking a tinfoil takeaway box on a piece of cardboard. 'And a tower of fear, a plunge of terror, and a pit of doom, and we can have those arcade games where you shoot things, like jelly eyes, and –'

'No.' Eric's face crumples as if he's in pain. 'Surely no one will want to go to something like that?'

'Everyone will want to go to something like that,' says Jacob.

They both look at me. I'm tempted to say nothing, but in the end I open my mouth and mumble, 'I suspect Jacob's right. People like being scared, a little, when they think things are under control.' Eric sags. 'And remember – this is about saving the bird reserve. Although we might have to keep an eye on the ghost train.'

'Billy and I will keep an eye on the ghost train,' says Flora Rose.

'Would you stop doing that!' I say, jumping and tipping an entire bucket of milk-bottle tops over the floor.

'Sorry, I thought you knew I was here,' she says. 'Anyway, I was always rather good at making things when I was alive. I'll help you. Well, I'll tell you what'll work and what won't. Now, is there any glue?'

There are hundreds of people in the town hall, all milling about, all chatting, and nearly all adults. Our model is standing on one side of the stage, and Whizzo's model is under a perfectly placed sheet on the other. Ours, even with Flora Rose's help, looks like a table heaped with household recycling and glue. Theirs looks as if it's going to be spectacular. It's bigger than it was in the library.

Everyone sits down and stares at us, expectantly.

The suit couple from the library step forward from behind the Whizzo table. 'Shall we go first, before the children?' Mrs Suit looks towards the mayor.

The mayor waves his hand airily, and goes back to checking messages on his phone.

'So,' says Mr Suit, smiling. 'We'd like to present Whizzo's updated plans for the upgrading of the current bird reserve.'

A photograph of the bird reserve appears on the screen behind. It's been carefully taken so that an empty drink can looms large at the front, along with globs of tar and half a plastic bottle. You wouldn't know it was a bird reserve – you'd think it was a recycling centre.

'An eyesore, I think you'll agree,' says Mrs Suit.

'Which is why we're pretty sure you're going to like this . . .'

As they speak, Eric goes pale and sinks back onto a chair. At first I think he's eaten something bad, and then I realise he's watching the woman peeling back the sheet over the model.

The entire audience gasps.

'Awesome, isn't it?' says the woman.

It's pin-drop silent in the hall as we all stare at the thing on the table.

It is awesome, but not in the way she means. There are the perfectly made white cardboard models you'd expect, like little buildings, and a roller coaster and trees, but then there are all these plastic birds. The kind of things that they sell in the toy shop: puffins and seagulls and robins and owls, all different scales and sizes.

Next to me Eric groans.

'So, welcome to Birdy World,' says Mrs Suit briskly. 'Yes, you're not going mad. We have changed the plan. Bunny World has become Birdy World! We thought, as you were so keen on your seabirds here, we'd transfer the theme to something more in keeping. Seagulls and – those sorts of things. So here,' she points at a white blob with wings, 'we have the Sandwich Tern serving sandwiches, and here the Puffin Play Club, and over here the Curlew Club for older . . .'

Some of the audience are shuffling in their seats. I can't work out if they're really enthusiastic and would like to get up and see more, or if they're appalled.

'So the other important issue is the relocation of the birds from this . . .' – another picture of the bird reserve flashes onto the screen, this time showing a rusty anchor and some bed springs – '. . . to this!' A picturesque, possibly airbrushed, photo of the Bywater Regis Lighthouse fills the space, seagulls wheeling above it in a blue sky and waves gently breaking over the rocks.

'As you know, the lighthouse is no longer manned, and is on its own rocky outcrop – perfect for the birds – although it is a little smaller than the area they have now. We –'

'It's tiny!' shouts someone. 'They wouldn't all fit on there – and there's no beach.'

'Ah, yes, we know there's no beach, but I'm sure the birds will adapt.'

'Adapt??!' shouts Mr Worthy. 'The Little Tern has been nesting on shingle for thousands of years – why would it adapt?'

'Any questions?' says Mr Suit.

'There were twenty-seven nesting pairs of Little Terns on the reserve last summer!' shouts Mrs Worthy. 'They're endangered, and there's no way they'd live on that rock.'

Someone else shouts, 'They can only nest in shingle! It would be a gross act of environmental vandalism!'

The mayor holds out his hands for silence.

'Please,' he says and turns to the Whizzo pair.

Mrs Suit is sweating now. 'And the ordinary seagulls will probably find somewhere to live quite quickly. We envisage the link road passing through this piece of marsh –'

'Where the Marsh Harriers live!' mutters Eric.

'And the car parks could be constructed on this piece of derelict swamp land –'

'The home of the Black-tailed Godwits!' shouts Mr Worthy.

'Thank you,' says Mr Suit. 'I think you should have a look at the model. It's self-explanatory.'

'Look!' says Mrs Suit, glancing towards the mayor. 'If you want your lido, you're going to have to put up with this.'

'The lido's great but we don't want to have it at the expense of the birds,' says Mr Worthy.

Mrs Suit raises an eyebrow and looks towards the mayor. 'Really? I thought the lido was very important.'

The mayor looks confused and drops his phone. 'Yes . . . no. I mean, obviously . . .'

'Admit it! You want the lido refurbished

because you share a roof with it!' shouts a man from the back.

A murmur goes around the audience. 'Of course,' says Grandma, standing up and addressing the mayor. 'It's all for your benefit, isn't it?'

'One hundred thousand pounds to restore the lido – and how much of that is the roof?' asks Mr Worthy.

Mrs Suit is smiling, although I don't totally understand why, and then she speaks. 'But the deal is signed,' she says, taking a piece of paper from her inner jacket pocket. 'Like it or not, Bywater-by-Sea is going to have a theme park – it says so here, signed, witnessed and contracted.'

Everyone stares at the piece of paper, and then, a millisecond later, everyone stares at the mayor.

He goes red, then white, then red again, and sinks his head turtlewise into the top of his jacket, so that only a pair of bright-red ears are visible.

We continue to stare at him.

'So everyone,' says Mrs Suit, brightly, 'I think Birdy World is going to replace bird reserve

– which is obviously a bit of a pity, but . . .' She shrugs.

'Not necessarily.' Eric stands up.

Mr Suit stares in amazement. Whether at Eric or Eric's hair is not clear.

Eric pokes me, and I poke Jacob. We all stand, reddening, as all the faces that were staring at the Whizzo couple stare at us.

'Instead of the bird reserve, we'd like you to use Mystery Smoke Island.'

The audience mutter, as if they don't know where we're talking about.

'The island about four miles off shore – the abandoned, haunted island?' says Eric.

People nod and look at us, waiting for something. I wish we had some photos.

'Well, Mystery Smoke Island is quite big,' says Jacob. 'And in a shocking state.'

'Much bigger than the bird reserve,' I say.

'Yes,' says Eric, unfolding a crumpled map and pointing to it. 'And it's already got lots of the things we need to –' He stalls, as if he's just noticed that everyone's looking at him.

'Build a ghostly theme park,' says Jacob, pushing the egg box that represents the Lilac Lake back into position and nudging me.

'It would make Mystery Smoke Island THE attraction in the South West. It would put Bywater-by-Sea on the map as a serious tourist destination AND it would prevent any development in the town itself,' I say – slightly too loudly.

'Yes,' says Jacob, butting in. 'And it could have its own sweet shop selling scary sweets, like headless jelly babies and screaming gobstoppers.'

'It would help the ferry companies and ensure the preservation of the existing, very satisfactory, bird sanctuary,' says Eric.

'It could open all night on Halloween,' says Jacob. 'We could have boats with pumpkins crossing the channel to the island.'

We look into the audience. People are screwing up their faces in doubt, sighing, checking their phones, picking their nails.

'It would be the only haunted-house themed park anywhere around. We could rename it

Nightmare Island,' I say desperately. 'And if you've been there, you'd know how convincing it would be.'

'Oooooooooh,' comes a long slow wail from nowhere.

Most of the audience jumps. The rest blink and turn up their hearing aids.

'Aaaaaaaahhghghghgh.' A strangled cry echoes across the ceiling and the lights flicker.

'Goodness,' says a woman in the front row, pulling her husband a little closer.

'Miiiiiaaaaooowwwwwwww.' Shipwreck James lets out a long mournful yowl.

'Oh woe is meeeeeeeeeeee ...' Flora Rose races around the chairs, leaving a shiver in her wake and the lights go out properly.

'Aaagh!' screams a woman from the back. 'Something just brushed my leg and there's nothing there!'

'I say!' says Grandma. 'Very good.'

The jam jar on the table turns silver and wobbles violently. 'Listen to them ...' squeaks Victor.

The audience gasp and stare upwards as a

purple blobby light appears in midair over their heads. It shimmers and flickers, wafting back and forth just below the ceiling. I can just make out Billy's hat and a big smile. It hovers for five whole seconds before he turns his mouth to a scream and swoops down over the seats.

'AAAAAAArghghghgh!' Mrs Suit grabs her bag and races for the exit.

'Aaaarghghghg!' chorus the front row, scrabbling over each other to get to the back of the hall – but before they get out of the doors, the lights flick on and the noises stop.

The escapees pause, look around at each other and no doubt feel foolish.

'Good show!' says Grandma, clapping furiously.

'Bravo!' shout Mr and Mrs Worthy. Slowly all the people find their seats and laugh and clap each other on the back, red faces all round.

'So?' I say when the chattering dies down. 'What do you think?'

The mayor puts it to a vote. 'Yes, yes, a vote then, everyone,' he says, looking up from his phone. 'We'll start by asking: who would like to see the development of Mystery Smoke Island as Nightmare Island theme park?'

I close my eyes. I can't bear to open them – in spite of Flora Rose's best efforts, they've probably all voted for the Birdy World park on the bird sanctuary.

A ripple of laughter runs through the room and I crank one eye slightly open.

They've all got their hands up, every single one of them. Grandma's got a huge smile on her face and is nodding at me.

Next to me, Eric's standing with his mouth open.

I feel 100 per cent good.

'Can it have a hall of mirrors?' whispers Flora Rose.

'I'm sure it can,' mutters Eric. 'Especially for you.'

We celebrate with Grandma's curdled cocoa and some slightly soft biscuits that Jacob jams into his mouth all at once.

Victor sits on a cotton reel and eats tiny slices of biscuit. He reminds me of a mouse, not just because of the way he eats, but also because of his colour. He's grey all over – his face and hands are grey, he might almost be covered in grey fur.

'So do we live on the island with the builders?' asks Flora Rose. 'Or stay here with you?'

'Island,' I say.

'Yes, island,' says Eric.

'Here,' says Jacob, prodding Victor with a cocktail stick. 'Hey – can you feel that? Are you still not quite a ghost?'

'Yes I can. Stop it, you imbecile!' says Victor, grabbing the end of the cocktail stick and giving Jacob a shove back. 'What about my castle? How do we know they're going to put one in? And how do we know it'll accommodate us as well as all the . . .' – he winces and flaps his hands dismissively – 'tourists.'

'Don't worry,' says Grandma, landing a warm fruit cake on the table. 'I've been asked if you can advise on the plans.'

'Yes, and we can be there every weekend and

every evening, talking to the men who are building it,' I say. 'AND they've said we can put all the scary things in ourselves.'

'So we can use real skeletons?' asks Jacob.

'And real blood?' asks Flora Rose.

'Um,' says Eric. 'We'll see.'

# Epilogue

It took six months for the theme park to be built. It was open just in time for Easter, and people flocked onto the ferries to visit the new, deeply terrifying Nightmare Island. The effects were universally acknowledged to be very special. No one could explain the howling that took place whenever anyone crossed the bridges, or the disembodied voices they heard, or the way things moved unexpectedly, or the extreme cold in the Tunnel of Ghastly Delights.

But although the dark, creaking castle was always terrifying, the tea shop was often cosy, the gardens bursting with beautiful flowers, the children's crèche warm and jolly and full of happy chatter. The island thrilled because it wasn't predictably ghostly – no one knew what to expect from one day to the next.

But the thing that made the visitors gasp above all else was the strange laughing girl's face that would appear suddenly in the hall of mirrors – one day there, the next, gone.

And at night, every night, the ghastly green glow of a television screen shone from a window high in the castle, accompanied by cackling laughter and electronic pings and whizzes. A voice would call, 'Yes! Yes! Yes! I've levelled up! I am the supreme master.' And sometimes it would shout, 'No one alive or dead can beat me – I am invincible!'

# Special thanks to:

Ben Donnelly
St Clements CE Primary School Year 5
Tina Brown
Lucy Hillsdon
Victoria Lloyd
Edward Lunn
Curtis Edwards
Nancy Wells
Alex
Asa Zirps
Isabella Morgan
Becky Gillan
Lucy Symonds
Rosie Davis
Alex Cole

Jasen Booton

Bettina Farkas

Beech Class & Miss Lloyd 2014 –
  Clent Primary School

Harrison Hartland

Elizabeth Baxter

Sapphire Wilkinson

Oldbury Park Primary School

Walk Like a Giant

Fluffy Unicorns – Pitmaston Primary
  School

Hiss The Creeper-Squid

# Contributors:

127

ANobodyZ

Aqrakinfenwa(pnp)

bentleypuppy(pnp)

book lovers

book monsters

Bookworm 121

Booty

candy crushers

Chocolate

Cookieclicker1

cool(fruitybookwormsyr5srwandfw)

coolcat(pnp)

coolkids

Crocodile (FruityBookworms5 CJ)

D3L1 2 G0(pnp)

dancer68

Dancesheep(FruityBookw'ms5BJ)

Dolphziggler(pnp)

Doodleduck

Dr Chopper

Duck(fruitybooksworms5EP)

Emerald buddy

EPIC DUDES

fab_fash(pnp)

Fancyfootball(FruityBookw'ms5NW)

Fluffy Unicorns 1 AC, LK, LS

Fluffy Unicorns 2 SJ

Fluffy Unicorns 3 CT, EG, ES, MR, OM

Fluffy Unicorns 4 BP

Fluffy Unicorns 5 ALM, MCS, RC, SG

Fluffy Unicorns 6 JLF

fluffyminion(pnp)

Fruity Bookworms Y5 AA, ACR, CJ, EBP, FW, JB, JP, LAT, LJH, MP, NW, SW

Fruity Bookworms Y6 AO, EJ, JG, RH, RR

girlonfire(pnp)

Glamarous girl (teenyweenyRH)

Headinabook (pnp)

HissTheCreeper-Squid

Huskies 18(pnp)

Husky 105(pnp)

ilikestuff(pnp)

Isapop

Izthewiz

Jellybean (pnp)

Karizma Kid

kittens

LB589

Lerwick Chatterbooks

Littlepuppy17(pnp)

lolipop(fruitybookworms yr5 lat)

Lollipop

madminecraftman595(pnp)

Masseyferguson(pnp)

minecraftmaniac97(pnp)

Minim

Minionboy9(pnp)

Miss Funface

mmmtpe aliens
moochaminion(pnp)
Name
page turners
Patchnpebbles
Piginspace
prettykitty(pnp)
Princesspeach(pnp)
Puppiesrcute123(pnp)
PurpleMonkeyJ-Cat
reachboy(pnp)
Scottot
Smallmessmaker
smashedpotatoes
Snowflake 123
sour sweets
Spacegirl
Spurs1882(pnp)
St Joseph's Juniors
Strawberry 4
sugary dohnuts
Tails cc
tas3303

Teenyweeny
The twits
Torres100[pnp]
Twinkle
Walk like a giant
Weinbag
Wolf10(pnp)
Wolfythewriter
zashasgirl(pnp)

# Star list

Cookieclicker1
Fancyfootball(FruityBookw'ms5NW)
Fruity Bookworms
Teenyweeny

# Superstar list

Booty
Isapop
Twinkle
Weinbag

# HOT KEY BOOKS

Thank you for choosing a Hot Key book.

If you want to know more about our authors and what we publish, you can find us online.

You can start at our website

**www.hotkeybooks.com**

And you can also find us on:

**We hope to see you soon!**